I sat in the corner, behind the last toilet stall and near the window. It was open, and the smoke from my cigarette floated outside so there was less chance of me getting caught if a teacher came in. I downed a shampoo sample bottle filled with my parents' vodka and started to feel better. Wiping ashes from my jeans, I reached into my bag and after pawing through scraps of paper, empty cigarette boxes, and odd butts from when my carry-along ashtray broke, I finally found a small, sharp piece of glass. I always kept sharp things in my bag for emergencies. Sometimes I carved designs—mostly crosses—but the way the day was going, I really felt like I might cry. I needed relief fast and this was how I was brought up. When I was little, my mother used to slap me across the face when I cried, "to give me a good reason," but once I got older, I found that wasn't enough. I began to use glass when I needed a reason to break down.

CROSSES

Shelley Stoehr

LAUREL-LEAF BOOKS

Published by
Bantam Doubleday Dell Books for Young Readers
a division of
Bantam Doubleday Dell Publishing Group, Inc.
1540 Broadway
New York, New York 10036

Visit us on the Web! www.bdd.com

Educators and librarians, visit the BDD Teacher's Resource Center at www.bdd.com/teachers

ISBN: 0-440-22780-1

RL: 5.6

Reprinted by arrangement with Delacorte Press

Printed in the United States of America

One Previous Edition

November 1998

10 9 8 7 6 5 4 3 2 1

OPM

*Dedicated to Mark Buhler,
Kathy Klock, and to my
parents for their
support.*

Chapter 1

"**We cut ourselves. Not by accident, we do it pur-**posely—and regularly—because physical pain is comforting, and because now it has become a habit. Like the drugs. These are, in fact, the two main things Katie and I have in common. They are how we met." This was my diary entry on November fourth, 1985.

When I met Katie I was fifteen. It was September of 1985, and I'd just started ninth grade. Before school I fought with my mother about the bologna I wasn't taking with me for lunch. I almost gave in and agreed to make a sandwich, knowing I would only throw it in the wire basket outside the school. But when I opened the plastic meat-keeper the smell made me want to puke. It didn't help that I'd sucked nearly a pint of vodka through a straw and straight up to my brain the night before. I clutched my stomach and scrunched my nose.

"It's bad," I said, "just smell it."

My mother reopened the plastic container. "Only because you've let it sit there for two weeks." She pushed my nose down near the pink, fat-covered, gross lunch-meat and I held my breath. When I couldn't keep from breathing anymore, I bolted from under Mom's grasp and escaped out the back door. At the end of the street, I vomited and felt better.

I was already sweating by the time I reached the end of

the next block. It was only the second week of school, and the weather was sultry. At least I'd managed to slip out of the house in my battered black sandals, instead of the socks and loafers my mother had bought and expected me to wear to school, no matter what the weather. It would be at least two weeks before it was cool enough to wear socks, and even then I wasn't thrilled about wearing loafers. Thank God they were black and would match my newly dyed hair.

I stopped in town to buy a diet Coke at the donut shop. Then, at seven forty-five, I shuffled into the brick school building and right away went to the bathroom to change from my parent-imposed conservative dress into a ripped fatigue T-shirt, jeans—on inside-out—and a long black vest. I knew the jeans would stick to my skin from the heat, but we weren't allowed to wear shorts at Babylon High.

I stuck safety pins everywhere and dangled paper clips from my ears. Finally, I spiked my hair, making it shiny with gel. Another girl came into the bathroom as I inspected myself in the mirror and I almost gagged. She also had gel in her hair, but the result for her was a big, poofy, feathered up-and-back lion's mane. My blue-black hair was short with bald spots where I'd cut too much. Spikes stuck straight up like pieces of broken glass. My shirt was green and black and dirty, the other girl's was pink with "Ocean Pacific" printed across the front. Her high heels made it difficult for her to stand securely, whereas my unevenness was caused by my hangover. I went into one of the toilet stalls so I could giggle without her seeing me.

When I first started dressing punk my mother freaked. I was barely fourteen, and I went shopping one afternoon with money I made baby-sitting. It was October and there was a Homecoming dance at school that night. I wanted to look good. Hand-me-down jeans with stovepipe bottoms and pink flowers embroidered on the back pocket wouldn't cut it. I couldn't afford real leather, but I saw a fake leather miniskirt. I bought it, along with a bright red T-shirt. "Screaming Hussy Red," Katie would call it a year later.

I got the effect I wanted. Everyone was shocked, even though my outfit was pretty bland in my eyes—the skirt, after all, came to mid-knee. It made me feel special, and I thought I looked pretty.

My mother wasn't home when I left for the dance, but she waited up for me later. She was watching TV in the living room, so when I came through the kitchen door, my father saw me first.

"Do you know how many naugas they must have killed to get the hide for that skirt?" he said, putting a jar of mayonnaise back into the refrigerator. I laughed and went into the living room to kiss my mother good night. She raised her eyes from the *TV Guide* and slowly took off her reading glasses. I'd suspected she'd be angry. Still, I wasn't prepared for the outburst I got.

"Do you *know* what you look like?" she said quietly, then yelled, "Look in the mirror! Go look in the mirror, then come back and tell me what you saw!" I didn't move. The TV's blue shimmer made her look older than her thirty-three years, and I thought, freakin' old bag—fuck you. I'm old enough to wear what I want, and there's nothing wrong with what I'm wearing.

"You look like a slut!" she screamed. I saw my father sneak past to the liquor cabinet, and hoped he would butt in and tell her to shut the hell up, but of course, he didn't.

"There's nothing wrong with what I'm wearing!" I said, "Amy Brown wore a denim miniskirt. Why don't you say something about her?" It didn't matter that Amy had actually worn jeans, I needed someone on my side and my sometimes-friend Amy was my mother's idea of a model child.

"There's a world of difference between leather and denim. And where'd you get the money?"

"From baby-sitting."

"Do I have to start hiding my wallet now, too?"

"The skirt isn't even that short, I don't know what you're complaining about."

"Don't ever let me catch you wearing that again."

I stood glaring at her, tears welling in my eyes. As I stomped up the stairs, I angrily refused to acknowledge my father when I brushed past him. Freakin' traitor. Wimp. I guess that's what happens when you spend forty hours a week sitting in a little cubicle looking at ledgers and a computer screen. You lose your backbone.

Slowly, my wardrobe hardened. I cut my hair short and started spiking it, started attaching safety pins and paper clips to everything, started wearing dark eye liner and heavy black mascara to make my bright blue eyes stand out like fishbowls. When I was drinking or high, the glassiness added to that illusion. My mother and I fought constantly about the way I dressed, so, rather than drive her to poking my eyes out with one of my own safety pins, I started carrying my clothes to school with me, and changing in the bathroom when I got there.

Now, a year later, I was still toting my wardrobe to a blue-green stall so I wouldn't look like a geek. Sometimes I thought that was my best subject: Warding off Geekness 101. I had to work harder than anyone else because instead of being blessed with beauty or wealth, I'd managed to be born with intelligence. Not enough to make me a blithering genius, but enough to make me sometimes act stupid and blurt out the right answer to a supposedly tough question. I tried to avoid doing that, but it could get real dull listening to some mop-headed teacher with sagging stockings whine, "Doesn't *anybody* know how Captain Ahab got his peg leg?"

The sound of thirty people riffling through their notes was so unnerving, I'd finally raise my hand and mumble the answer, pulling on a safety pin and trying to look like I hadn't really done the reading, but somehow this one answer had just come to me. If it weren't for my clothes and my attitude, I never could've gotten away with it. As it was, I still wasn't sure it was working. Fourteen years of being a geek is hard to fix.

Still, I could try. After changing my clothes in the bathroom, I colored my lips with soft black eyeliner and lit a cigarette in the stall. I kept the door open a crack, so I could see if anyone came in. Unfortunately, when a hallway aide did slip in, my sneakiness didn't help me any. I was the only one in the bathroom, and Miss Clairol swore she smelled smoke, so I was snagged. Protest was useless—it didn't matter that she hadn't seen a cigarette, I was written up, and would probably get detention.

The day got worse. I went to math class first period, and got back the first test of the year. Scrawled in red ink across the top of the ditto was, "85% — Good!" Good? I pressed my fingers hard against my desk. Good? This was the lowest grade I'd ever gotten in math. I mean, my father was an *accountant* for Christ's sake. It was in my *blood* to know numbers and shit. I crumpled the test, and without asking permission I took the bathroom pass and left the classroom, my army bag slung over my shoulder and my fingers clenched hard on its strap as I tried not to cry.

I sat in the corner, behind the last toilet stall and near the window. It was open, and the smoke from my cigarette floated outside so there was less chance of me getting caught if a teacher came in. I downed a shampoo sample bottle filled with my parents' vodka and started to feel better. Wiping ashes from my jeans, I reached into my bag and after pawing through scraps of paper, empty cigarette boxes, and old butts from when my carry-along ashtray broke, I finally found a small, sharp piece of glass. I always kept sharp things in my bag for emergencies. Sometimes I carved designs—mostly crosses—but the way the day was going, I really felt like I might cry. I needed relief fast and this was how I was brought up. When I was little, my mother used to slap me across my face when I cried, "to give me a good reason," but once I got older, I found that wasn't enough. I began to use glass when I needed a reason to break down.

Puffing hard on my cigarette, I squeezed my eyes shut and pulled the glass up my arm again and again. Suddenly I felt like I wasn't alone anymore, and opened my eyes. In front of me stood a girl with funky clothes, a ton of jingling bracelets, and incredible long blond hair with little spikes on top—Katie. I blushed almost as red as the blood which was beginning to surface on my arm. For a few seconds, we only stared at each other. I'd seen her around, but never spoke to her much. She hung out with a different crowd, the so-called "dirt-bags." I'd always wanted to be a part of her group, but like I said, despite my clothes I was stuck with a "good girl" image.

Finally, I said, "Hi."

"Hey, do you have an extra cigarette?" she asked.

I gave her one, and my lighter, too, and she sat down next to me on the tiled floor already littered with butts and ashes. I was still nervous because of the blossoming cuts on my arm. I think she read my mind because she smiled and showed me her shoulder, which had a scabby cross about an inch long carved into it.

Chapter z

At lunch I went outside to smoke a cigarette. Our school had junior and senior highs combined in one building. Out at the designated smoking island across the street from the cafeteria exit, I got to hang out with a lot of seniors, which was cool. It was especially cool because only ninth graders and up were allowed to leave the school building for lunch. This was only my second week at the smoking island. Even so, today I didn't bother trying to socialize with any of the older girls because I saw Katie off to the side. I joined her, and she smiled.

"What's up?" I said, throwing my hip out to the side and slipping a finger into the waist of my jeans. I almost wished I could fling my hair back like she did, but decided running my fingers through my black spikes was sophisticated enough.

"Not much," she answered. "Do you smoke?"

At first I looked at her a little confused—I had a cigarette in my hand. What did she mean, "Do you smoke?" Then I noticed she'd made a ring shape with her forefinger and thumb and was holding it to her red-frosted lips. I realized she meant, "Do I smoke weed." I grinned, trying to look cool.

"Fuck yes," I said. "Do you have any?" Meanwhile I was thinking to myself, oh shit, now you've done it. You don't even know how to hold a joint. She's going to spot your ignorance in a second. Stupid.

Katie pulled me by my arm around the back of the tennis courts, her many-colored bracelets jangling on her wrist. When we got there, she took out a baggie of weed and some paper. She began rolling a joint.

I took a deep breath and said, "Actually, I lied. I've never smoked before. I would of, but I never had the opportunity. Sorry. I can go and leave you alone now, if you want." I was redder than Katie's lipstick.

Katie didn't say anything. She licked the joint shut, handed it to me, and took a brush from her black leather purse. She stroked the long blond back of her hair, leaving the shiny, spiked top alone. Then she put the brush away, looked at me with muddy-brown eyes rimmed in green liner and mascara, and said, "So. There's a first time for everything, right? If you want to try it, now's the best time, 'cause I'm the best teacher. Here, gimme. I'll take the first drag, and you just watch me. You suck really hard, like this." She talked while she was holding the smoke down, then handed the joint to me. "But don't close your mouth too tight on the end, or you won't get anything through." she said.

Watching her reaction to see how I was doing, I inhaled deeply.

"When you start choking, you've got enough smoke," said Katie. "That's it! Good! Hold it in, hold it in! Cover your mouth when you cough, it makes the smoke go back in."

After three hits, I had to sit down. It was like my first cigarette head-rush, only worse. All my limbs were like Jell-O, but I didn't feel high, not that I knew what high should feel like. I wasn't laughing like Katie was, and I still felt pretty much in control of my senses. The tennis courts still looked green, and the sky was still blue.

"You never get high your first time," said Katie. "You just feel funny. Next time it'll be in your blood. Then after one hit you'll be flying like me. Or else you'll just float. That happens sometimes too. That's when you know you're really stoned—when you feel like you're just going to float away like a big hot-air balloon."

Katie laughed so hard then, she started to choke. Swat! I hit her on the back as hard as I could. She laughed even harder, but stopped choking at least.

Still giggling, she reached a fingerless studded glove into her big, black purse and flipped out a Heineken bottle cap. She started making a small cross on the back of her hand. I watched, fascinated. She's just like me! I thought. We both started giggling at the same time. Maybe I *am* high! I thought. I couldn't stop laughing. Somehow the pin-sized droplets of blood bubbling from Katie's hand were the funniest thing I ever saw. The little hairs on the back of her hand stood out like tall blond grasses in a tiny red sea. Katie, sputtering with laughter, fell onto her back and pulled up her shirt to expose her belly and show me a K-shaped scar next to her navel.

"That's so my boyfriend, when I get one, always knows who it is he's sleeping with," she explained, laughing. "So he doesn't yell out any other girls' names!"

I pushed my green-and-brown short sleeves up to my shoulders. My arms were covered with many different shapes and designs.

"So *my* boyfriend *doesn't* know who he's sleeping with," I said. "He doesn't understand it. He thinks all he has to do is say so and I'll stop. He thinks he can take care of me."

Katie nodded. Then we start showing each other all our

various scars—some still fresh and scabby, some red and some glaring white against our barely tan skins. As fellow cutters, we didn't have to explain why we made most of the scars.

I told Katie about the time in seventh grade when my friend Tom and I sat at a lab table in science, way in the back of the room. I forget what the lab was—something using Bunsen burners, I think. I wasn't into the punk scene yet, I was just an ordinary, geeky newcomer to junior high. In the cafeteria the day before, I'd noticed two older girls at the table behind me scratching their arms and competing for who could scratch the longest. One girl got two hundred scratches. I was sitting all by myself and feeling kind of lonely and bored, so I tried scratching my own arm, but stopped after only twenty scratches because it didn't seem right, doing it without a reason.

As I sat at the lab table in the back of the science classroom, it dawned on me that because Tom and I had finished our lab early and had nothing to do, there was a reason to make the scratches. Since Tom was even geekier than I was, and I knew he had a crush on me, it was easy to convince him to play the game. First it was my turn. Tom scratched back and forth across my forearm with his fingernail, and I looked away because it's harder if you see the cutting happen. Even though it was only my first time cutting, I knew the rules. When Tom got to one hundred and sixty-three scratches, I told him to stop, and it was his turn. As I scratched him, I looked at my own arm, which burned now, and was glazed with blood and pus. Tom quit at one hundred and sixty-four. Not wanting to be beaten, I made him scratch me twice more. Although the first hundred sixty-three times hadn't hurt much while they were being done, the last two were very painful. Tom made me scratch him twice more, putting him back in the lead. I hated to give up, but the game was getting too painful. It wasn't fair that he got to go first, but next time I would. Besides, it was only a game.

Tom and I didn't want to pull our sleeves down over the cuts because we thought the fabric might stick to the pus and would hurt to rip free later. But we should've been careful then. Tom passed our teacher's desk on his way to the bathroom, where he was going to wash his arm, and Mrs. Schwartz noticed the red streak of blood.

"Can I see your arm?" she asked, and Tom, not thinking, lifted it for her. An instant later, he yanked it back to his side, but it was too late. I cringed, and so did Mrs. Schwartz.

"What's that?" she demanded.

Tom shrugged.

"Thomas, I asked you what that was on your arm. Show it to me again. Thomas, I want to see it. Thomas, what *is that*? Did *you* do that? Who did that?"

I prayed he wouldn't gesture to me. Oh God, I thought, it was only a game, please don't let me get in trouble. I won't do it again, I promise.

Tom looked at the floor and mumbled, "It was only a game, I won't do it again, I promise."

"It's not a very funny game!" she yelled. "Who else is involved in this?"

He refused to answer. Good friends are like that—they'll die before they rat on you. Even after Mrs. Schwartz telephoned his parents, he didn't tell on me.

Back in the world of ninth grade and Katie, I wasn't laughing anymore. I was almost crying, remembering two years ago when cutting really was only for fun. I didn't seem to need it then, but all of a sudden I thought, I can't stop! Then I thought, I don't even want to.

"What are you so worried about?" said Katie, pushing thick fingers into her bangs and squirting them with hair spray. "You can stop cutting whenever you want, just like me. It's just that you don't want to, because it's good for you. It keeps you from being overwhelmed by all the shit around you."

Chapter 3

Part of the reason Katie and I became best friends so soon was that we were so honest with each other. By the end of our first week hanging out together, I felt like I knew her completely. On the third day after I'd met her we went outside, behind the tennis courts for lunch, got stoned, and told each other everything we could think of to tell in the half hour before lunch ended.

It was another hot day, like the day we met, so Katie rolled up her tank top and tucked it into her bra. I did too. As she bent over to get her lighter out of her purse, I noticed rolls of fat gather around her belly, but when she sat up again they mostly disappeared. She was a little chunky, but overall had an amazingly good figure, considering her life-style.

"Mostly at home I sit and watch TV, or sit outside in the backyard smoking pot," she said, handing me the joint. "My mom's not home much, she mostly comes in from school—she's a teacher—changes her clothes into something slinky, and goes out on dates."

I exhaled smoke and handed back the joint. The weed must've been really strong because already my senses and powers of observation seemed heightened. I hadn't noticed how much bigger Katie was than me before, but suddenly her hand looked almost twice the size of mine. "How tall are you?" I asked.

"Five ten," Katie answered, her hand over her mouth to keep the smoke in.

"I'm only five two," I said. "I get my size from my mother."

Katie pulled out a brush from her purse and stroked her hair absently with it. "I get my height from my father, I think. Well, my mother's kind of tall, but she's a lot thinner than me. My father's more my size overall, or at least he was last time I saw him. It's been two years."

"Do you miss him?" I asked.

Katie laughed. "No way. He was a mess. He worked in the city for an engineering firm and he used to get so drunk after work he'd fall asleep on the train coming home. Lots of times he'd slip off the seat to the floor and the conductors wouldn't notice him lying there when the train stopped in Babylon. The train would go to the yard, and my father would still be passed out under the seat. He'd wake up and call at like three in the morning. After a while my mother refused to go pick him up so he'd have to walk home. He'd fall asleep on the couch and I'd wake him when I got up for school."

I picked at a scab on my ankle for a few minutes and didn't say anything. My head was cloudy from the pot, and it took a while to formulate a sentence. "God," I said finally, "I thought *my* parents were bad! I mean, they drink a lot and can really be assholes sometimes, but at least they drink at home!"

Katie giggled and made a funny face at me.

"What's so funny?" I asked.

"You are! Here, have a cigarette and lighten up." Katie handed me a Marlboro and her green Bic. "Chill out and don't take everything so seriously or I'll never tell you anything about my family again!"

I stuck my tongue out at Katie and she tickled me under my arms. I kneed her in the stomach to get her off of me, and we both rolled around on the grass wrestling for a while, until it dawned on us that lunch was almost over and we both had cravings for sour cream and onion potato chips.

In only a month, Katie had completely accepted me for what I was, which was amazing to me. In fifteen years, my parents had yet to accept anything about me. But, I thought as I walked to school, I didn't really need my parents' acceptance anyway. Brrr! Even though it was only early October, it was *cold* out! Hard to believe that only a month ago I'd been lying out on the grass with Katie, soaking in the sun. That's the problem with the Northeast—it gets way too cold, too fast. For God's sake, there were still leaves on the trees! And the problem with suburbia, I thought, looking at the quaint little houses, is that it's so dull. And people still wonder why their kids do so much dope!

When I got to school, after the homeroom bell rang, I met Katie in the second-floor bathroom. It was becoming like our own private bar. I brought vodka I stole from my parents' liquor cabinet. They didn't notice because I replaced what I took with water.

Every morning I'd sneak downstairs to breakfast at six-thirty and before pouring milk into my Cheerios would quietly click open the cabinet door and lift the vodka—or sometimes it was brandy or rum—out over the necks of the other bottles. I'd pour half a paper cup full, then pour half a paper cup of water back in. I knew my parents would finish the bottle before more than one paper cup of water had been substituted for booze, and since they typically mixed their drinks with water anyway, there was no way I'd ever be caught. Anyway, me and my paper cup would then hurry to the bathroom to pour the vodka into my old shampoo sample bottle. My hand would be shaking and my face wet with sweat, because any second my mother would be down making coffee.

I didn't think of the replacing booze with water trick on my own, I read it in a book about a teenage alcoholic. That was my hobby, reading books about teens in trouble. I wasn't allowed out at night during the week, I couldn't stand to sit and watch TV with my parents, and my homework never took me more than an hour to finish. I filled in the extra hours before bed with stories about drug addicts, anorexics, and alcoholics.

For Katie and me it wasn't alcoholism though, it was boredom. Anyway, I brought vodka and Katie brought straws. Using them, we sucked down the vodka in fifteen seconds, and already felt woozy. That was the idea—to try to get blasted on as little drink as possible. We still had time to pass a cigarette back and forth between us before the bell rang and we were late for our respective classes.

Second period Katie and I both had gym. This particular October Monday we were so wasted we were almost having a good time. Usually, we hid and tried to get out of doing anything in class, but suddenly we wanted to play badminton.

Katie skipped up to a guy with unkempt greasy blond hair and thick glasses. "Tim," she said, leaning against his arm.

"Look out!" he yelled, trying to free his arm so he could reach back and hit the birdie which was whizzing over his head. Katie fell backward and landed on her ass.

"I'm sorry, are you okay?" said Tim, bending over her and looking like he just ran over his dog.

Katie lay still with her eyes closed.

"Oh God! Mr. Winters!" Tim looked toward the gym teacher, and Katie sat bolt upright.

"Forget it, Mr. Winters," she yelled to the approaching instructor, who scratched his bald head and happily returned to watching the cutesy girls on another court bob up and down in their pink shorts as they tried to hit their birdie.

Katie pushed herself to her feet and gestured to me. "Tim, can me and my friend play?"

"Sure, sure. You're sure you're okay?"

We batted the birdie around for a while, best we could, laughing like crazy, especially every time Tim clapped his hand to his pimply forehead in exasperation. After a while, we got dizzy, and went into the weight room to lie down.

"That fuckin' birdie was giving me a headache," said Katie. "Fuck."

Katie had her Walkman, which had two headphone jacks so we could both listen to her Led Zeppelin *Coda* tape. Even though we were both punkers, we liked Zeppelin and Floyd a lot. More than most punk bands, actually—except for Bowie, our favorite. Even with Bowie, we didn't like anything he'd done lately. We considered ourselves seventies punkers, stuck in a conservative eighties world.

We lay down on adjoining benches with the headphones on and spaced out until the end of class. We were still so trashed when the bell rang, we accidentally forgot the Walkman and tape in the weight room. By the time we found our way back through the smelly gym to get it, it was gone. Easy come, easy go. Katie stole the fucking thing anyway, so who cared? Katie only cared about the bump she got crawling under the bench press to see if the Walkman was hiding under there.

Happily, we used the lost Walkman as an excuse to get out of our next class. Of course, instead of spending a half hour looking for it, like we said we were going to, we sneaked into the locker room and napped on benches. Not too comfortable—they were only three feet long and a foot wide each—but what the hell. A half hour later, I threw up in the bathroom, and we returned to class.

As time wore on, Katie and I discovered we could get away with anything. Actually, Katie always knew this. I was the one who was just learning, which was why I could get away with even more than her. No one expected me to do anything wrong, but they watched her. Besides, I had pretty good grades to back me up, while she was just getting by in most of her classes. She only did enough work to squeeze through the system each year. Not that she was dumb. She read an awful lot, and better quality stuff than I did, but she still wouldn't read what was assigned to her. It was against her ethics to do assigned work. I still did most of my homework, but like Katie, I weaseled out of doing a lot of stuff. Like for example, my classwork, which was impossible to do when I was spending most of my morning hours drunk in school.

Unfortunately, because we never got caught, Katie and I started to get careless. We didn't brush our teeth before going to class, and we didn't hide what we were doing from our classmates. Even though they were our ages, they were mostly straight, so our drinking shocked them.

One day, less than a week before Thanksgiving and in gym class again, Katie and I sat in the weight room with some people from our third period biology class. Not a good idea. One girl was my lab partner. She put her big Italian nose in my face and sniffed.

"You've been drinking," she said.

"No shit, Sherlock!" said Katie and we both giggled.

One of the other girls laughed, too, and asked how much we'd had to drink.

"Oh, who cares?" said my lab partner. "Don't make them seem any cooler than they already think they are." She turned to face me where I sat on the leg-press bench. "I think you're stupid alkies, and I think you're going to fail the quiz next period."

I ignored her, and answered the other girl. "We had half a Hellmann's jar of gin today. A little variety—usually we have vodka in shampoo bottles. And no way am I going to fail the quiz. I studied for a whole fucking hour last night. I know it back and forth."

Katie snickered. "I don't know it at all, but I never know anything anyway. At least I'm consistent."

The bell rang then, and after changing our clothes, we went to biology. My God, I thought, stumbling into the room and noticing the jars of gross-looking stuff on the front lab counter, what the hell is this? Katie was next to me, laughing.

"What about the quiz?" I asked Mr. Smith, our teacher.

"Oh," he answered, barely looking at me, "I'm postponing that until tomorrow. We're dissecting frogs instead. You're late. Hurry and sit down."

I slid into my seat at a lab table in the front of the room. My lab partner grinned widely, showing her big, white, buckteeth. I stuck out my tongue. Still, I thought, even if she is a bitch, I'm lucky—Katie's partner was absent. Boy is she in trouble, I thought.

Katie's frog was pregnant, so when she cut it open it was full of shiny black eggs. "*Maggots!* There're maggots in my frog!" she cried from the seat behind me.

Both of us burst into giggles. Tears slid over my cheeks, I

was laughing so hard. I nearly slit my lab partner's throat as I turned around with a dissecting knife in my hand to examine Katie's frog.

Mr. Smith raised his bushy eyebrows at us, but only warned us to quiet down and do our work. We would've been fine then, if I didn't get stupid. Just playing, I carved a little cross in the palm of my hand with my dissecting knife, leaving my lab partner to clean up our disemboweled Kermit. It was neat to cut without feeling pain, and I liked watching the tiny bit of blood surface. It fascinated me.

I was so absorbed in cutting, I didn't notice my lab partner staring at me until she blurted, "That's disgusting! That's *sick*!"

I mimicked her. "That's disgusting, that's sick. Fuck you."

Great idea. Paula didn't take abuse well. "No, fuck *you*," she said, loudly enough that other people, including Mr. Smith, started tuning in to what she was saying. "Why don't you drink a little more—then you can *really* start a good fight! Get away from me, sickie!"

As she finished her attack, thank God, the bell rang. Katie and I whisked up our books from the black lab tables and tried to slip out the door unnoticed. But Mr. Smith grabbed us by our shoulders with two bony hands and pulled us back into the room. We rolled our eyes and followed him into his office.

He slowly shut the door, sat on the edge of his desk and glared at us. "How dare you come to my class drunk," he said.

We shrugged. Katie rolled her eyes again and ran her fingers through her hair. I lightly elbowed her in the waist, trying to shush her.

"How do you think this makes me feel, as a teacher?" He

was looking only at me, like Katie no longer existed for him. "Do you think this is acceptable behavior? *Do* you? Do you think your classmates think it's acceptable? I think they're very disappointed with you. I don't think most of your classmates find this cool, do you?"

Because I was sure it was what he wanted to hear, I shook my head and said, "No. This is only the first time. We just wanted to try it."

Katie popped a piece of gum in her mouth and blew a bubble. I cringed, but Mr. Smith didn't notice. His eyes were fixed on me. Always *me*. Always *my* fault. I dug the nails of one hand into the opposite arm.

Mr. Smith sighed and fingered his short, bristly beard with one hand. "Why here? Why now? Do you know how much trouble you might be in right now? Do you know what this little experiment might cost you?" I noticed a piece of food hanging from Mr. Smith's mustache.

Katie butted in. "It's no big deal. We were only trying it this once."

"And why do it? For adventure? Are you bored?"

"We're sorry, please don't report us."

"Are you so bored you have to drink?"

"Can we go now?" Katie persisted.

"I'm surprised at you, Nancy. Katie—I might expect this from her, but not from you."

"I have a test next period, can I go?" Katie shifted her weight to her other hip.

"You have so much going for you, why are you trying to louse it up? Are you having troubles at home? Something I can help you with?"

"There's nothing wrong with us," I said. "We just wanted to try it. We didn't think. We're sorry. Are you going to write us up, or what?"

Mr. Smith leaned forward, put his feet on the floor, and his head in his hands. Then he sat up straight. "Because of your good record, Nancy, I'm not going to report either of you this time. You know, I *could* send you down to Mr. Grossman's office for a breath test, and the cops would come, and your parents would be called. But I trust that this will be the one and only time you do this. I'm probably crazy to let you off. If you end up dead from alcoholism at age twenty, I'll regret this for the rest of my life."

"It won't happen, trust us," I said, "We won't drink anymore. I don't even like the feel of it. Thank you, Mr. Smith."

"We'll keep this between us, but don't let it happen again. I mean it—if I even suspect you of drinking before my class, I won't even ask for an explanation—you're going straight downstairs to Mr. Grossman's office. Are you still under the influence now?"

Katie and I shook our heads.

"Here, here's a pass for your next class. Go on."

We left the office, not looking at each other because we were afraid we might burst into laughter. What a jerk! It just proved, once again, that with good grades and a charming smile you could get away with anything. As I approached the door, I accidentally knocked into the side of a desk, then careened sideways into another. Katie laughed. So much for not being under the influence anymore!

For the rest of the day, we bragged about what we did. Actually, I did most of the bragging. Katie didn't have to brag—everyone expected her to be drunk or stoned even when she wasn't. But I made sure for the whole of my next two classes before lunch to let it slip to just about everyone what happened.

Lounging sideways across two chairs in the cafeteria during study hall, I even pulled the eight-ounce mayonnaise jar out of my army bag again and conspicuously dumped the last quarter inch of gin into my plastic cup of black coffee. My black-painted lips spread into a wide smile as the mouths of my good-girl friends dropped open. But that wasn't the important reaction. What made me smile wider was the thumbs-up I received from Rob, a long-haired, skinny dirt-bag seated at the table next to me.

Suddenly it was lunch. Booze was great for making the day go fast. I was pretty much sober by then, and I really wanted to go out behind the courts to smoke a joint with Katie. Unfortunately, I remembered at the last second that I had to meet Mike, my boyfriend of nearly a year, at his house for lunch.

If I hadn't been feeling a little horny from not seeing Mike for almost two days, I probably wouldn't have gone to his house. I would've called and made up a lie about having to get a homework assignment done or something. Since I'd been hanging out with Katie, it seemed like sex was my only reason for staying with Mike. Before Katie, Mike used to be the only person I had to talk to, so I considered him kind of my savior. I was pretty sure that was a lot of the reason why he liked me—I made him feel needed.

I remembered when we first met. I was at a party at my friend Amy's house. Her parents were away, and everyone was drinking heavily. It was the first time I'd gotten drunk. Since I didn't know anyone but Amy at the party, I sat in the corner of the couch and gulped blackberry brandy until I could hardly sit up. Feeling sick to my stomach, I stumbled to the bathroom but someone was already using it. I threw up on the door, then sank to the floor and began to cry, I was so embarrassed. Next thing I knew, Mike was lifting me under my armpits and carrying me outside. He cleaned me up and sat with me until I felt better. Later he took me home, and the next day, he asked me out. Four days later I lost my virginity and got my first hickey, right above my breast.

Part of what I liked about Mike was that he was popular, so I got to go to a lot of parties where there was almost always free beer. In the beginning, Mike drank at least as much as I did, but after a while he slowed down and I became the only drunken slob. This put a strain on our relationship, but I was still good in bed. I let him do anything he wanted to me. Besides, I made him laugh. After one drink, I became less shy, and my sense of humor came out. Sometimes I was sure Mike and I were madly in love and would get married as soon as we were both old enough. Other times I wasn't so sure we were in love, but I still believed we'd get married and live happily ever after, if only because we satisfied each other's needs. I was good in bed and he took me to nice places. What a deal.

You'd think I was still drunk, the way I acted when I got to Mike's house. I bounced into the freshly vacuumed living room, rubbing my teeth with my forefinger one last time so Mike wouldn't taste cigarette smoke. He was lying across the couch in very-blue jeans and a red flannel shirt, open at the neck and exposing thick chest hair. That was one of the advantages of dating a senior—he was at least way past puberty, while at least half the guys in my class had yet to sprout a single hair above the waist. Mike was a man, even if he was boring as shit. I mean, red flannel just can't cut it, unless the sleeves are ripped off.

Maybe it was Mike's ultranormalness that made me plop down on the edge of the flowered couch, kiss him lightly, and blurt, "Wait until I tell you what fucking Mr. Smith did to Katie and me today . . ."

I knew Mike would be mad about what I did, yet I told him everything. If I were smart, I'd have kept my big mouth shut for a change. But of course I didn't.

I could've been sitting next to Mike on his couch, playing with his hair and telling him how beautiful his arms were because they were so big and muscular. His forearm was about the size of my calf. He could've been kissing my neck, but instead I briefed him on what happened in Bio. He snapped up from his pseudoseductive position and angrily smacked my arm with the back of his hand.

"That was fucking brilliant!" He sat still for a minute, then punched a small, frilly pillow. "Damn it, don't you have any brains?"

"We didn't get in trouble."

"Don't you even give a shit about *me*?"

"Don't you think it's kind of funny we didn't get in trouble?"

"You must not care much about me, if you keep doing shit like this. You know you're eventually going to end up being grounded, and then what?"

"We get away with everything so easily, isn't that weird?"

Mike growled. "Would you just shut up and listen? I want you to stop with this garbage. You'll end up getting grounded, and I won't be able to see you. Am I asking so much? Aren't I worth a little straightening out?"

At first I glared at him, arms folded across my safety-pinned and torn black T-shirt. Then I nodded and smiled—that charming smile that works almost every time. "Okay, I'll stop. I don't want to not be able to see you."

I leaned forward and fell across Mike's chest. Unbuttoning his shirt, I curled my fingers through his wiry, dark chest hair. I kissed the inside of his elbow. He tried to be stern, but in a few seconds, he bent to kiss me, no longer angry, of course. If you're good in bed, you can get away with a lot, too.

Chapter 4

December and January passed fairly uneventfully for me. Even Christmas was not exciting, since Katie and her mother went to California to visit her aunt for the whole vacation. Mike gave me Swiss Fudge Cookies as a joke and I gave him a sweater. No big deal. New Year's I got drunk and stoned on the joint Katie gave me for my Christmas present just before she left for California. On January third, school began again.

Since I was scheduled to meet Mike for lunch only on Monday, Wednesday, and Friday, I got to spend two lunches a week with Katie. Of course, Mike hated that. He said she'd get me in trouble. I didn't much care, which was why every other day, Katie and I went to The King's Wok, a Chinese restaurant in town, to drink the free tea, eat the free noodles, and smoke weed in their bathroom. The days I ate at Mike's became my recuperation days.

Mike's house always amazed me, probably because it was so clean. His mother worked full time as a hairdresser, yet somehow she managed to dust and vacuum every day. The kitchen and bathrooms always sparkled, and I never saw a book or magazine out of place unless Mike was studying at the dining-room table. It was all very different from my house which was cluttered with old newspapers, clothing thrown anywhere, dirty glasses, and enough dust to make the modern, white Formica furniture look gray.

Mike always went home for lunch, since he lived only two blocks away from the school. As a senior, Mike had a double lunch period, so he'd usually be there waiting for me. We hardly ever ate. There were better ways to spend a half hour. But one day in February, just before Washington's Birthday, I was totally starving. It was so cold out, I almost called and told Mike I wasn't coming. All I wanted to do was grab a slice of soggy pizza in the cafeteria.

But I went anyway, and got to Mike's house shivering like crazy. That morning, Katie and I hadn't been able to drink—we hardly ever did since we were caught that time. Walking against the wind to Mike's house, I wished we had. Maybe then I'd have been warmer. Mike opened the door first knock, thank God. He was wearing an oxford button-down shirt and jeans, and he smelled fresh, still wet from the shower. The scent of Brut, my favorite after-shave, was strong.

"Didn't you go to school this morning?" I asked, dropping my heavy overcoat to the floor and pushing off my shoes.

"No, I had homework I didn't get to finish last night. Hundred pages of *Frankenstein.*" He stepped forward across the mauve shag and wrapped his thick arms around my waist. "Have you lost weight?" he asked, kissing my neck softly.

"Some," I said, glad that he noticed. "I'm a hundred and four, isn't that good? But my legs are still a little fat."

"They're not. They're perfect. Come here." Mike picked me up and carried me into the brown and navy kitchen. On the table were a white tablecloth, candles, fancy napkins, silver, and two peanut butter and jelly sandwiches. Mike lowered me gently to my seat. I smiled broadly, unable to think of anything to say until he brought out his own homemade chocolate chip cookies for dessert. I was overwhelmed, which was rare for me when I was around Mike.

"Can I sit on your lap?" I asked sweetly. When I was comfortable, I said, "I love you."

He said he loved me too, and of course I believed him. I always believed what he said, even though I think I knew deep beneath all my safety pins and scabby cuts that our whole relationship was based on sex and lies. I thought they were all *my* lies. And that made me alternately proud and disgusted.

But sitting on Mike's lap, I tried not to question "us," although I did briefly wish again that I'd gotten drunk with Katie earlier. That always made everything easier. After inhaling a sandwich, Mike started kissing my neck and shoulder, cheeks and hair. I tried to continue eating, but it was impossible to concentrate on anything but Mike's tongue and teeth. He did this to me all the time—and I wasn't complaining. Maybe I should've been, because it was bad to allow myself to be ruled by a man simply because of what he could do to me physically, but then, wasn't I ruled by cutting, too? That was physical, and yet not nearly as enjoyable as sex.

Mike's tongue was in my ear and his fingers in my hair, absently separating clumps that were stuck together with styling gel. I pushed back the kitchen table and swiveled around on his lap, so that I could face him and wrap my legs around his belly. Grabbing a handful of my hair, he pushed my face into his and roughly kissed me. While we bit each other's faces, I unbuttoned Mike's shirt and pants. He slid off the chair to the floor, at the same time pushing my shirt up above my breasts. We rolled all over the place, and eventually did it right there on the floor. I didn't enjoy myself completely because I was thinking about the safety pins in my clothes, which were strewn across the tile. What if we rolled onto one and it opened?

Oh shit, I thought, looking at the clock. I pushed Mike off of me. "It's late. I have class in three minutes," I said, standing and pulling on my fake leather pants.

He bit my ankle.

"Ouch! Cut it out, that hurts!" But I was giggling too, because it didn't hurt too much, and I didn't want to offend him. Whatever turned him on was okay by me, I mean there was no sense in being a prude. If I were, he'd find someone else in a minute, and where would I be then? It was kind of funny, too. Sometimes it would dawn on me that Mike and I weren't so different after all. Looking at him, no one would ever believe his sexual habits were so rough, and I felt special knowing even just this one secret.

Because of the ways Mike responded sexually, I couldn't understand why he didn't appreciate my cutting. Still, understand or not, I tried to hide my cuts from him, which could be tricky sometimes. Other people weren't so hard to fool, especially in winter, since I wore long sleeves. Mike was the only person besides Katie who saw my skin from November to March. Wouldn't you know that just as the weather started improving, about the second week in March, was when I made my worst cuts to date.

I was lying in my bed at night, silently cursing my parents for being so goddamn noisy when I had school the next day. Fucking shitheads, I thought. Can't they find some other time to fight? I've got a fucking English test at nine o'clock, and I have to listen to *this*? Jesus Christ!

In a half hour, the shouting seemed to have stopped, which was good because I had to use the bathroom and only the one on the first floor worked right. I didn't want to go through a battle zone, but I was practically bursting, so I wrapped my green terry-cloth robe around me and tiptoed downstairs to the living room. The battle wasn't over. My father was at the front door, wearing his checked bathrobe. His hair was mussed, and there were three long fingernail scratches across his cheek. He didn't notice me at first. I heard my mother crying, and saw that she had her hand stuck in the door, grabbing at my father's robe as he tried to shut her out of the house. I didn't want to be involved, but I couldn't stand my mother's whimpering. I pulled my father away from the door. He was so shocked to see me, he didn't resist. Then I let my mother in.

Falling onto me, she cried, "He's trying to kill me, he's trying to kill me! I think my arm is broken! I have a concussion!" She smelled of alcohol, and I pushed her away from me in disgust. Then I knew she was drunk, because she'd never stand for that if she were sober. She'd smack me until I couldn't see straight.

My mother's face was covered with blood and for a moment I was scared, but then I noticed a small cut on her forehead, dripping so it seemed like her whole face was bleeding. "See what that monster did?" she whined, clawing at my arm with pink-painted nails. She seemed even smaller than she was at five-foot-two.

"She fell down the stairs," said my father, quietly. He looked exhausted as he poured whiskey into a glass at the kitchen counter. "She wants to go to the hospital, I said, 'go ahead,' and now she expects me to drive her there. I told her to hitch."

I didn't want to hear any of it. I went to the bathroom, and when I came out, my father was turning the bolt on the door, and my mother was standing on the porch, banging and screaming. Her arm went through one of the glass windows at the top of the door, and as I headed upstairs, I heard her scream that her wrist had been slashed and she was going to bleed to death. Police sirens were whirring in the distance.

I'll show her slashed wrists, I thought, reaching into my night table drawer and taking out a big piece of broken glass left from when I broke a vase of flowers over my head a few months before. Flipping off the light, I bit my lip and pressed the glass hard into my wrist. I kept saying to myself as I dragged it up and down, fuck you, fuck you, fuck you. Eventually I started to cry, dropped the glass on the floor and fell asleep.

I didn't realize how deeply I'd cut until the next morning, when I woke to find my wrist stuck to a sheet with dried blood. There was an awful lot of blood there and I wondered how I'd explain it to my mother when she took my sheets to wash them. Probably say I had a nosebleed. Carefully, I pulled my wrist free and put a gauze pad on it because it had started bleeding again, a little bit. Jesus, I thought, I'm lucky I'm not dead! I must be fucking crazy! I was supposed to see Mike at lunch, and even if I wore long sleeves, he'd certainly see my wrist and be royally pissed off. Shit.

I had an idea. I put an elastic wrist brace over the bandage, and if anyone asked, I'd say I fell and twisted my wrist.

Everyone, even Mike, believed me. Only Katie knew the truth, and only she understood why I did it. It wasn't a suicide attempt, it was an escape from everything awful. When we cut, we're in control—we make our own pain, and we can stop it whenever we want. Physical pain relieves mental anguish. For a brief moment, the pain of the cutting is the only thing in the cutter's mind, and when that stops and the other comes back, it's weaker. Drugs do that too, and sex, but not like cutting. Nothing is like cutting.

Chapter 5

Katie and I kept smoking weed in The King's Wok at lunch twice a week, and Katie's birthday was no exception. March nineteenth, Katie turned sixteen and I even took off my wrist brace for the occasion. I knew Katie would appreciate the scabs.

As we lit up in the restaurant bathroom, it would have been easy for us to get caught—there wasn't even a lock on the door—but as Katie said, "What's life without risks?"

"The suburbs," I answered before inhaling deeply on the joint. We both cracked up laughing.

"What a great excuse!" said Katie, "You see, Mom, we get fucked-up so we won't become permanent fixtures of the suburbs."

I clipped the joint and sang, "We're movers, we're shakers, we're damn good drug-takers . . ."

We left the bathroom, and for the first time since we'd been frequenting the restaurant, splurged and ordered meals. While waiting for them, we went back and smoked another joint in the bathroom. Five minutes later, we returned and our meals were ready but it was already twelve-thirty. Only ten minutes were left before French class! Katie and I burst into giggles.

One of the wonderful things about weed is that you can eat like crazy. We put our mouths at the edges of our plates and scooped the food straight down our throats, laughing the whole time. It's a wonder we didn't choke. I never knew broccoli and chicken could be so easy to swallow, but it slid right down, no problem. With five minutes to go, we got our check from a little Chinese dude who looked very upset to see us. I bent to take money from my purse. As I sat up again, the broken pin which was holding my shirt closed fell out, and following it came my chest. By the time I noticed, the waiter was looking right at me, his face a damn good match for his red bow tie. I quickly yanked my shirt closed again, and Katie and I hurried from the restaurant, giggling again.

Running up the stairs to class, I suddenly remembered the test we were having in French. I was sure we were doomed, and as I wrote responses on my answer sheet, I was even more convinced. I couldn't make any erasures either, since one hand was fixed to my blouse, holding it together. When I tried to erase, the whole paper moved, which was very funny to me, but didn't help my exam any. I kept wondering if maybe Mrs. Spencer could tell I was stoned.

Two days later, we got our tests back. A ninety-eight! Katie got a ninety-five! Wow! I thought it wasn't fair of us to keep this to ourselves—we should market the idea—sell joints at an increased cost to people who wanted to succeed in French classes.

Sometimes Katie wasn't able to get any weed—she was always the supplier. I gave her money. So we took ups. There was a senior girl Katie knew who sold us little white pills with green flecks on them that she called Christmas Trees. They were five for a dollar, so we managed to do pretty well. I don't know why we took them, since they weren't very enjoyable. We ended up sitting in class almost too hyper to stand it. All I wanted to do was go outside and run around the block three or four or a hundred times.

The first day we took them was really bad, so you'd think we'd have sworn off them right away, but we didn't. It was the same—what's life without risks?—again.

It was early April when we popped the pills in the pizza place next to The King's Wok that first time. We felt that each new drug should be taken in a new setting. My wrist had finally healed to thick, white scars, which meant I could wear short sleeves again as long as I was careful. Though the scars blended in with my pale skin, they were raised and therefore a little noticeable.

Since being caught drinking by Mr. Smith, Katie and I tried to stay straight in the mornings, so at lunch, between bites of pizza, we each took three Christmas Trees. Before going back to school, we smoked half a joint too. We didn't realize how screwed up we were until halfway through French class. I looked at the blank sheet of notebook paper in front of me and knew that I'd just written two paragraphs of a composition using the wrong end of my pen. I looked at Katie and noticed she was shaking, unless it was only my eyes.

In seventh period, we had art together, and we started to come down. Walking into the room, Katie grabbed my arm and I yelped. Her leather glove felt like a dead starfish and I was afraid it would suck out all my blood. Some starfish do that. We sat in the back of the room, hands clenched to the edge of the table. One of our friends, Jessie, came in, and I shakily called her over to us. She looked puke-green, so I didn't look at her when she talked.

"Wow," she said, "you guys are really fucked up!"

We didn't answer her, but concentrated on sitting still.

My butt muscles were clenched so hard they were quivering. In fact, my whole body was quivering.

Jessie reached over and wiped the sweat from my cold forehead. "Don't drink any coffee, whatever you do," she said.

"What do you think we are, stupid or something?" Katie snapped.

Jessie only laughed. "Try drinking a lot of water, stupid." Then she left.

As soon as I could, I released my fingers from the edge of the table and got up to go to the fountain. Katie screamed softly. She was afraid to be alone, and when I thought about it, I was too. So we went together, holding hands the whole way. Two hours and probably as many gallons of water later, we felt better just as Jessie had predicted, and wondered what we'd been so worried about. Still, we were more careful after that. Never more than one pill at a time.

Chapter 6

When we couldn't get ups or weed, Katie and I experimented with aspirin. It was perfect, because we could get away with doing it in the mornings, and Mr. Smith couldn't catch us. Maybe it was psychological, but we felt high after swallowing five or six. Once, in English class, I even sniffed the contents of a Tylenol capsule. I did it only in fun, on a dare, and regretted it instantly. Gasping, I held my nose, which burned like I just squirted acid up it. It continued to hurt for a good two hours and during that time, I wondered *how* people could snort coke. Still, it made me a little high. The next day, Katie and I bought a bottle of Tylenol.

Tylenol sniffing remained a joke to us, but we took aspirin ingestion seriously. Not in the sense that it became an addiction, but we believed it worked, and we did it a lot. It was cheap, legal and easy to get away with. And we figured since it could never hurt us, what the fuck? That was before I got sick, and had to take aspirin for medicinal reasons.

I got a cold at the end of April, complete with fever and chills. But I knew I couldn't stay home from school because I wouldn't get to see Mike at lunch, and I wouldn't be allowed to baby-sit at night. I needed the money to buy a dress for Mike's prom, only two weeks away. Not that I really wanted to go anyway, but if I didn't, Mike said he'd go with someone else. Worried sick he'd leave me, I decided to go, and to look terrific. Luckily, my mother said she'd pay half the cost of the hundred dollar dress I'd chosen. That left me with a bill of fifty dollars, of which I only had twenty-five. If I could stay well enough to baby-sit, I'd earn ten to fifteen dollars more.

I thought if I took some aspirin, I'd be fine. I probably wasn't that sick anyway. But I was afraid I'd built up a resistance with all my recreational use of the drug, so I took three instead of the prescribed two pills. That might have been okay, except that then I took three more. And three more. And three more. Between each class I took three aspirin, and by two forty-five I felt awful. It was like being in a bubble, everything seemed so far away. I figured it was because my ears were ringing so much. I felt sick to my stomach, but every time I escaped to a bathroom and bent over the toilet, I couldn't make anything happen. Worst of all, I was shivering, though sweat was pouring over me. As I walked home with Katie I imagined it must've been the fever.

"I feel shitty," I said. "I better take some more aspirin when I get home or how will I be able to baby-sit? I almost don't even want to."

"You should've stayed home today, idiot."

"Couldn't."

"Could so. And how many aspirin have you had? It seems like every time I saw you, you were swallowing some at the water fountain."

Mentally, I counted what I'd taken throughout the day, and I was shocked when I finally figured it out. "Twenty-four, I think."

"Twenty-four aspirin in about eight hours. Real smart. You fucking schmuck! No *wonder* you feel like shit!"

I didn't know what I should do then. I couldn't tell my parents what happened because they'd get mad. Besides, they wouldn't let me baby-sit either, and I had to buy that dress. Luckily, I had a first aid book at home, and Katie read to me about aspirin overdoses. I had all the symptoms in order, except for the last three: "blue fingernails and lips," "coma" and "death."

The book suggested drinking a lot of tea for the tannic acid, but I couldn't right away because my mother was home. I had to wait until after dinner, when I was baby-sitting. I promised to call Katie later and tell her how I was doing.

At dinner, I felt like I was going to die, no exaggeration. My mind kept wandering, no matter how hard I tried to focus my attention on my parents' conversation. Not even bothering to try talking, I concentrated as best I could on keeping my head from swaying. I wished my ears would stop ringing, it was giving me a headache. And it wasn't like I could take two aspirin to make it go away. The food made me want to vomit, and I hoped my parents didn't notice my sweating.

Finally, it was seven o'clock, I was alone with a nine-month-old baby, and I could drink some tea. I put four tea bags in a chipped cup and drank it straight down, my lips barely able to stay fastened to the ceramic. In the other room, I heard the baby crying in her playpen, but the sound seemed far away, and hardly bothered me.

When my tea was done, I felt guilty so I went to check the baby. I wished she would get tired and fall asleep. I had enough to worry about without having to contend with her. But I picked her up anyway, and rocked her. Carrying her upstairs, I breathed heavily, still suffering from shortness of breath, though I was starting to feel better. I nearly fell from dizziness, but I leaned against the wall until I was breathing almost normally and seeing straight again.

For bad overdoses the book suggested that the victim be fed activated charcoal. But my lips and fingernails were still normal so I thought I was okay. Besides, where would I have gotten freakin' activated charcoal? I sat staring at the television, hardly aware of what I was watching, and prayed. "Please God, I don't want to die. I know sometimes it seems like I do, because of the cutting and stuff, but I don't, I really don't. If you let me live, I won't pretend I'm going to kill myself anymore, I promise."

By ten o'clock, I felt better. So much better, I called Mike. "Guess what?" I said. "You're going to think this is really funny—I do. You know how I felt really sick at lunch today? Well I kept feeling worse all day, and thought I must be *really* sick, but it turns out it was only an aspirin overdose! I'm such a jerk! Only *I* would do a stupid thing like that, right?"

Mike was silent for a minute. "Are you okay?" he asked, not laughing.

"Of course I am! It's not that serious an overdose. I read in *Home Health Emergencies* to drink tea for the tannic acid, and did. Now I'm fine. I felt awful for a while, but now I'm much better. Listen, want to come over and visit?"

Mike said he was on his way. For a brief moment, I wondered if I told him about the aspirin overdose just to get him over there to see me. No. Mike would've come over anyway, so why would I have to lure him? I loved when Mike visited me while I was sitting, because except for at lunch, we rarely got to see each other. I had a very strict curfew.

When I let him in, he stared at me for a few seconds,

looking worried, before putting his arms around me. "Nancy," he said, "you look terrible!"

It was true, I was still sweating a lot, but other than that, I was fine. I almost said, "You don't look so good yourself—what a dumb shirt!" Instead, I decided to just get him out of the blue Lacoste as soon as possible. "I'm fine. I'm better now," I finally said.

Before pulling Mike's shirt over his head, I went upstairs to check on the baby one more time, to make sure she was still asleep. She was. I came back downstairs with my shirt off. I knew I must be crazy, because if Mr. and Mrs. Krebbs came home early from their dinner party, I'd be humiliated, and in a *lot* of trouble. Well, the shirt was just for effect anyway. I put it back on, and rolled it up to my neck. Mike ogled me for a minute, then grabbed me and started kissing. He stopped briefly to ask, "Do you think we should do this—I mean, you're sick and all," and I said I wasn't sick anymore, but to wait a minute while I found a towel or something to put on the couch so we wouldn't accidentally stain it.

We made love quickly. Our clothes weren't even all the way off. That way if anyone came home, we could pull up our pants and Mike could disappear out the back door. Still, rather than take any more chances than necessary, as soon as we were done, I made Mike leave. He was satisfied that I was okay. So was I, and I called Katie to tell her so.

"You're a fucking jerk," was all she had to say.

Less than an hour later, my ears started ringing again. Worried, I turned off *Newhart* and looked in the bathroom mirror. First, I noticed two purple hickeys on my neck. Damn it! I picked up a comb and tried to get rid of them. Then I noticed my blue lips, and put down the comb. I was beginning to get really scared.

Still, I kept my cool because I knew I could take care of myself. I made myself another cup of tea with four tea bags, and calmly resumed combing out the blood in my hickies. Soon I felt better and could actually hear the TV without any ringing again. But I drank another cup of tea just to be safe. I went upstairs to check the baby. She was awake, trying to scale the bars of her crib, so I stayed with her, singing "Puff the Magic Dragon" to put her back to sleep and to soothe my nerves.

Chapter 7

Seeing Katie at lunch wasn't enough for either of us, especially since Katie had only a few friends from her neighborhood. Since Christmas she'd been hanging out with Mike and me at his friends' houses and going to parties on the weekends. I liked that because whenever Mike got too dull, Katie and I could get sloshed together and ignore him.

About the time of my aspirin overdose, I noticed she was talking about Mike's best friend, John, a lot. I didn't question her, I waited until she was ready to tell me she had a mad crush on him. The Sunday after Mike's prom, she was.

I was tired and hung over from the prom, so I didn't go out partying again with Mike that Sunday. Instead, I biked to Katie's house. In all the time I'd known her, I'd never been to her house, so I was a little nervous. I wondered if her mother was really like she said. As I pulled in front of Katie's aluminum-sided ranch house, I noticed her mother standing on the front stoop in her bathrobe, although it was one in the afternoon, kissing a thin man with glasses who stood a foot shorter than her.

By the time I'd parked my bike in the backyard, Mrs. Meenan and her date were gone. I knocked on the front door.

Mrs. Meenan opened the door and ushered me into the house. "You must be Nancy," she said. "Come sit down in the kitchen, I was just making pancakes. Are you hungry? Katie's in the shower, but I know she'll be right down. Go on, sit anywhere. So, how's school?"

"It's fine," I said, sliding into one of the vinyl chairs at the table. I put my elbow on the table for a second, but quickly pulled it back. Smiling uncomfortably, I wiped the sticky pink stuff from my arm with the smelly dishcloth Mrs. Meenan gave me.

"Would you mind wiping the table, too, while you're at it?" she asked. "It's jelly, I guess. It's hard to say. Sometimes I just get so busy I can't find time to clean up around here, and gunk piles up. Oh, and call me Dawn."

Well, Dawn, maybe you and my mom can start a bad-housekeeping club, I thought as I watched her spatter pancake batter all over the stove and onto her blue bathrobe.

Mrs. Meenan looked like she was going to keep chattering, but luckily Katie came running down the stairs and interrupted. "Hey," she said to me, "how's it going? Wow, pancakes! I'm starved!"

Katie sat next to me at the table and pulled an ashtray closer to her, offering me her open pack of Marlboros at the same time. I declined, and was amazed that Katie was going to light a cigarette in front of her mother.

"Do you smoke, Nancy?" Mrs. Meenan asked, glancing over at us.

"Of course she does, Ma!" Katie answered for me.

"Do your parents let you smoke?" Mrs. Meenan asked then.

"*Ma*, you're embarrassing me! Of *course* they let her. Whaddya think she is, a two-year-old?"

"Katie, you don't have to get bitchy with me. I was only asking because I don't want to get in trouble with anyone's parents. Go ahead, Nancy, smoke."

Because it sounded more like an order than an offer, I took a cigarette from my purse and lit it. Katie smiled at me and rolled her eyes.

Soon the pancakes were done, and Mrs. Meenan sat at the table with us to eat them. They were doughy and undercooked, and some were burned on one side. I pretended not to notice and stuffed large bitefuls into my mouth.

"So, Nancy," said Mrs. Meenan as she helped herself to more pancakes, "do you have a boyfriend?"

"Ma."

I nodded.

"Do you have sex with him?" Mrs. Meenan asked, and got up to pour herself a cup of coffee.

Katie was pissed. "Ma, cut it out, okay? Just don't start."

"Well, Katie dear, I only want to know what's normal for girls your age. I see that it's normal to smoke cigarettes. I want to know what else is normal about you so I don't have to worry. Nancy, do you do drugs?"

Katie was turning red and looked like she was going to cry. I wondered if I should leave.

"Just shut up, Ma!" Katie yelled as she pulled me toward the stairs. "Shut up or I'm never asking anyone over here again! Shut up or I'm leaving!"

As Katie and I hurried up the stairs to her room, her mother screamed, "Don't you run away from *me*, little girl! You come back down here! I'm talking to you! Katie!"

Katie leaned against her closed door and slid down to the floor into a pile of dirty underwear. "Sorry," she said, "I thought she might behave for once."

I shrugged my shoulders. "Whatever. All parents are weird."

"Not like my mother," Katie said, shaking her head.

I shrugged again.

She got up and opened her top dresser drawer. "You're right," she said. "Who cares, all parents are weird. If you want to smoke, this is the ashtray."

I lit a cigarette and went over to the dresser where Katie was standing, flicking her cigarette into a clay ashtray that sat in the midst of papers, pens, and pieces of garbage. The ashtray had overflowed, so ashes and cigarette butts were mixed in with the rest of the junk.

"So, how was the prom?" Katie asked.

"It was okay, I guess. I don't remember much of it. We went to a party at some girl's house beforehand and got sloshed. Plus the limousine had a full bar. The music was pretty bad, and my shoes hurt my feet. Other than that it was okay." I yawned.

Katie sat on her floor amid the dirty clothes, books, dishes, and scraps of paper. She didn't say anything for a minute, then asked quietly, "What was John's date like?"

"John didn't go. I thought he was going to, but I guess he decided it was too expensive, or he was too chicken to ask anyone." It was all I could do to keep from asking why Katie was so interested in John's date, but I didn't have to.

Getting up and standing facing the mirror, Katie put her cigarette out.

"John is kind of cute, don't you think? I think he is," she said, pushing gel through her hair and pulling it up into spikes.

"Ask him out."

"He's not my type, and you know it. Christ, I think he's more freakin' straitlaced than Mike!"

"Mike's not that straight, really."

"So he's an animal in bed. That doesn't mean shit, you know. He's still a stiff, and I'll never understand how you

guys can stand each other. I wouldn't be able to take it—
that's why I can't go out with John. But he is cute. I
wouldn't mind a good screw."

"I'll tell Mike to tell John you're interested in a good,
long relationship."

"Don't you dare!" But she didn't sound too threatening. I
thought it would be great if she started seeing John. Then
we could hang out together all the time, and she wouldn't
have to feel like a third wheel. And I wouldn't have to feel
guilty about making her feel that way.

The next day at school I told Mike, who told John. I was
impatient, so when I saw him at the end of the day, I
asked, "So?" I leaned against the locker next to his.

He raised an eyebrow, and I laughed. It's exactly the
same What-the-fuck-could-you-*possibly*-mean? look I always
got from Mike. Besides Katie and I, I'd never known two
best friends as well matched as Mike and John. They
looked almost like twins—both with neat boyish haircuts,
simple, rugged attire, well-built bodies with hints of beer-
bellies, pale complexions. The only noticeable difference
was that John was about three inches shorter than Mike.

Their personalities, too, were alike. Both had great senses
of humor, except about drugs and things like that, which
Katie and I found hilarious. Still, they were always faithful
—to friends, lovers, family, pets, whatever. No matter what
values or feelings have been hurt, they'd stick by the ones
they loved. That was important for me and Katie. And they
did a good job taking care of things, like us.

"So, what do you think?" I asked John.

"About what?" he asked, avoiding my eyes and opening
his notebook.

I smacked his arm, and he shrank back, laughing and

nearly dropping the notebook. Papers fell out and slid across the hall floor. "About *Katie*!" I said.

"She's nice, I guess."

"Do you think she's pretty?"

"I'm not blind."

"Do you want to go out with her?"

"Maybe. When I decide, I'll ask her, not you, okay? Go bother Mike, I have to go to work."

I rolled my eyes. "So does he. Fucking workaholics, the both of you. Okay, go. I better hear good things from Katie, though. Call her tonight."

"Maybe."

"Don't forget."

"I don't have her number."

"Her number's in the book. Last name Meenan."

"I lost my phone book."

"Don't be a prick."

John did call Katie that night, and that weekend was their first date. Katie told me they fought about the scars on her arm, one of which was fresh and hardly free of its scab. She tried to explain to him that she was bored, that's all. It wasn't anything serious. Like Mike and my seventh grade science teacher, John was upset. But Katie promised not to do it again, and John let it go at that.

They slept together for the first time, and that fixed everything. Then they were peachy together—not a care in the world. I took her with me to the clinic to put her on the pill. John, like Mike, hates having to buy condoms. He refuses, and Katie and I refuse to give blow jobs, except on special occasions. I mean, why should we? What do we get out of it? It's disgusting, it's not even fun—it's uncomfortable. Only on Mike's birthday, or if I'm taken to dinner and bought a bottle of wine and permitted to smoke in the car on the way home, only then will I give a blow job. Guys get what they pay for.

Chapter 8

Come the beginning of June, the weather was sunny and beautiful. If either Katie or I had owned cars, we probably would have cut out every day to go to the beach. We did cut out of one class and sneak up to the school roof to lay out on the hot tar, but it wasn't the same as going to the beach. The beaches are probably the only good thing about the whole of Long Island.

Just thinking about going to the beach gave Katie and me two serious cases of spring fever, and Mike and John were real pains in the asses about it. On school nights I wasn't allowed out, but I was used to getting around my parents' dumb rules so it shouldn't have mattered. I still should have been able to see Mike every night if I wanted to. But he refused to let me, not wanting me to get in trouble. John wanted to hang out with Mike, and Katie refused to hang out with both Mike and John without me. This left Katie and me both home alone Sunday through Thursday nights.

It was almost funny, Katie and I dating Mike and John. When we hung out with other people, they always said, "How can you go out with such stiffs? You're so wild—don't they stifle you?" Of course they did! But that was part of the attraction.

Maybe Katie and I should've been stifled more than we were. Maybe we needed a couple of stiffs to keep us from swinging right over the edge. John and Mike kept us from getting so wrapped up in ourselves that we went crazy. Besides, we loved them, and they loved us. We knew they did because they told us so, and we knew we did because we talked about it a lot, and what else could it be but love?

In spite of Mike and John's disapproval, Katie and I sneaked out a lot. Often we didn't do much, but just sat around, examining the crosses in our skins and thinking up new excuses to give.

The second Wednesday night in June was probably the most beautiful night since the summer before. The sky was clear and sparkling with stars, the temperature was about seventy degrees, and a salty breeze was blowing in from the bay. Katie and I learned that Mike and John were going to a party at their friend Matt's house. We couldn't resist, and planned to meet at the end of Matt's street at twelve-thirty.

I had to stay awake until twelve-fifteen, when I had to leave, since my alarm would wake my parents, but I couldn't leave my light on or make any noise. Usually while waiting to sneak downstairs I sat up in bed listening to my Walkman, but it was out of batteries, so this time I tried reading instead. I hid with my book and lamp under my quilt so that my parents wouldn't notice a light on in my room.

At eleven o'clock my parents still hadn't gone to bed. They were probably arguing or something. Maybe they were watching a late movie. Shit, I thought, putting down my book. What should I do? What if they don't go to bed early enough for me to meet Katie by twelve-thirty? I mean, I knew Matt's street, but would I be able to find the house?

Fifteen minutes later my parents stumbled up the stairs

to bed. At twelve they seemed to be asleep—I could even hear my father snoring—but I didn't want to be hasty, so I waited until twelve-fifteen before tiptoeing down the stairs and through the living room and kitchen to the back door. Every time a board creaked, I stood still for a count of fifteen. I didn't hear any movement from my parents' room, so I kept going. As soon as I was outside, I ran to Matt's street, just in time to catch Katie before she gave up on me.

"I thought something happened. I was worried," she said.

"Old farts . . . wouldn't . . . sleep . . ." I panted.

"Catch your breath," she said, pulling a lighter from her purse, then a tissue, which she handed to me. "Then wipe the sweat off, and smoke this with me." She held up a thick joint that glowed white under the glare of the streetlight.

We smoked, and were soon laughing about how awful I looked, all sweaty and red. My Garfield nightshirt was hanging out beneath my sweatshirt, and I didn't have a single safety pin to put in my ear. Katie lent me a paper clip, which made me feel a little better. To cover the smell of pot so Mike and John wouldn't give us any shit, we lit cigarettes and swallowed a shot of rum each.

The party was crowded, but Katie and I weaved through the throngs of people and finally found Mike and John together in the kitchen, playing quarters. There was a slutty-looking bitch leaning over Mike, her tight pink dress exaggerating her almost nonexistent breasts, but I was too high to be bothered. Looking at Katie, I laughed at her puckered-face imitation of the tramp until tears ran from my eyes. Mike must have heard me, because he looked up, raised his eyebrows, and sort of smiled, looking pretty damn surprised. Katie and I floated into the circle of people around the table, and sat possessively on our boyfriends' laps.

I lost track of time watching the game and trying to keep Mike's groping hand out of my crotch, but it must have been less than an hour before he suggested we leave, and next thing I knew I was on the couch at his house. How nice. The music was too loud at that party anyway. But I hoped my parents wouldn't notice the hickeys on my neck the next morning.

Mike walked me home about an hour later, leaving me at the end of my block, so if I got caught, at least my delinquency wouldn't be connected to him. By that time I was no longer wasted, but I was still buzzed enough to slow my reactions. I went to the back door of my house, not thinking to check if any lights were on, which they were.

As the door creaked open, I saw the light in our living room and heard my father's recliner as he sat up. Quickly, I shut the door and ran behind our garage. I jumped over the wire fence into the backyard of the house behind us. Since I still had my nightshirt on beneath my clothes, I took off my jeans and T-shirt and removed the dangling paper clips from my ears, leaving them under a bush. Then I returned to my own yard.

The light in the family room went out and I should've waited, but I panicked. I assumed my father knew it was me, trying to get in, and was going upstairs to check my room. I knew I'd be in *big* trouble if he discovered that I'd stuffed clothes into my bed to make it look like I was sleeping in it. That made the act premeditated. So I banged on the door, and he soon answered it. He really didn't know I was out because he looked shocked and asked what I was doing there.

Since I had a history of sleepwalking, and I was dressed

in sleepwear, I answered dreamily, "I had to milk the cows."

He asked if I'd been sleepwalking and I responded with a blank stare. He was convinced, and I got to go to bed. Close call.

This didn't keep me from continuing to sneak out at night, but it made me more careful, at least about sneaking back into my house. Often, my father was up, so when I saw the light I waited outside until he went back upstairs, usually at about three A.M., and then I went in. The big, empty scotch glass and full ashtray told me what he'd been doing. I hated sitting outside, with dew making everything damp and a little chilly despite the warm season. But it was better than when I got home and no one was up. Then I was never sure if my father had maybe been up and had just gone to sleep, or if he'd been in bed for a while and would be getting up any second. It made coming in a little nerve-racking.

Chapter 9

The last week in June, before school officially lets out and finals begin, there's never anything important to do, and everyone's just itching to get out of school and into trouble. Katie and I were no different, so one day we told our art teacher, Mr. Lyme, that we needed extra time to work on our projects. We weren't doing anything in French class, so couldn't he please write us passes to get us out of it? That way we could work straight through two periods.

Mr. Lyme raised his eyebrows and laughed. "Right," he said. "My two hardest working artists, how could I turn you down?"

"Oh, come *on*," we whined until he signed the two slips of paper we'd thrust in front of him.

We should have been happy with getting out of French class, but instead, we got greedy. It was important to us to keep the old motto in mind—what's life without risks?

Katie knew of a deli near school that didn't proof anyone, especially her since the owner was after her body. Instead of getting pizza or Chinese food at lunch, we went to the Crossroads deli, Katie jiggled her breasts at the owner for a few minutes, and we walked out with a six-pack of Meister Bräu. As we turned away from the register to leave, we bumped into Mr. Lyme's T.A., Joan, who was buying herself a Yoo-Hoo. For a second, the three of us stared at each other. I instinctively put my arm over the beer I was toting, but instead of putting it back, at least until Joan left, I let Katie pull me to the door. Joan watched from the register, but she didn't say anything, so who cared?

It was late, so there wasn't time to drink before returning to school. Katie stuffed the beer into her backpack and, giggling, we marched into Mr. Lyme's room. He smiled "hello" and left to buy his lunch. "Back in fifteen," he said. "Work hard!"

As soon as we saw him disappear around the corner into the stairwell, we took the bathroom pass, and ran down the hall with the backpack swinging between us. In the bathroom we crowded together into the space between the stalls and the window and each popped open a can, but before we could drink even half of it, the door opened. Out the window with the open beers, zip the pack shut. Oh great. It was Joan, of course. I'd recognize her high-necked white blouse and baggy BonJour jeans anywhere. Shit. Shit. Shit.

She grabbed each of us by the backs of our necks, and pushed us out the door. I hoped the safety pin holding the neck of my shirt together would open and impale her palm. Katie tried to leave her backpack behind, but Joan noticed it and we had to bring it with us.

Mr. Lyme was waiting in the hallway, his hands on his hips and his face beet-red with perspiration. Boy, were we in trouble, because there was our very favorite biology teacher, Mr. Smith, standing next to Mr. Lyme, his lips pressed so hard together, you couldn't see them in his facial scruff. And damn it, he looked like he'd spilled his story too. Bastard.

We were left alone with Mr. Lyme in his classroom. "We weren't going to drink it here," Katie argued.

Mr. Lyme raised an eyebrow. It made a perfect V over his eye. Then he growled, good and loud.

"We bought it for someone else—they were meeting us there," Katie continued, and I nodded.

Mr. Lyme raised his other eyebrow. "Girls," he said, "I'm pissed." Then he started spouting all the "how's" like, "How could you? How dare you? How do you think *I* feel?" His voice crescendoed louder and higher in pitch and he started talking in circles, or so it seemed to me.

I stared at Mr. Lyme without flinching because I wasn't hearing what he said until he stopped, breathed deeply, and grabbed Katie and me each tightly by our wrists.

"Ouch!" said Katie.

"You're in big trouble, young ladies. Big trouble!" he said.

That got my attention. "Bullshit!" I said, snapping out of my fantasies and trying hard not to cry. "You don't *have* to turn us in! We were only trying it! We're not the only ones!"

"Why is everyone ganging up on us?" Katie asked.

Mr. Lyme sighed and looked as gentle as he was able, considering his anger. "Just cut it out, okay? You know I hate this, but I don't see any other way. From what Mr. Smith tells me, there's a problem here."

Mr. Lyme looked like he was breaking, like maybe with a little more whining from Katie and me, we could slide by, so I said, "What kind of problem? We drank once before. That makes this only the second time. Since when is that a problem?" I gripped the bottom of my army bag with one hand and could feel the edge of something sharp. I just held it—I think it was probably glass—running my fingers over the canvas I pulled taut around its sharp edges.

"This is twice that we know of. There could be hundreds of others," said Mr. Lyme, his color deepening again. At least he'd let go of our wrists.

I put on my saddest face. "We won't ever do it again, promise. We never tried beer before. We just wanted to try it."

Pounding his fist several times on his desk, Mr. Lyme looked ready to explode, but gradually he took some deep breaths, and, looking at his fingernails, said, "I'll make you girls a deal. Let me have the beer, and I won't turn you in, this time."

I looked at Katie and our eyes widened. It was hard not to smile, and I let go of the piece of glass in my bag. We whimpered at Mr. Lyme a little more, to give him the impression that he was getting a good deal and making us repent and suffer. Then we tried not to skip out of the room. In the hall, we shook hands energetically.

"We are *so* cool," said Katie.

"I know," I answered, running after her to the bathroom. We smoked cigarettes and returned to Mr. Lyme's room for our regular art class, where we painted diligently for nearly a half hour before he called us into the hallway.

"I've been thinking," he said, "and I've decided I was a jerk before. I have to call your parents." Katie started to cry —not much, just a little wetness in the corners of her eyes, and I was shaking. My *parents*! I wanted to be tough, but my eyeballs were like rivers, and there was nothing I could do to stop the water from flowing.

Mr. Lyme sadly tugged at his chin. "What else can I do?"

"You could forget this happened!" Katie shouted.

"And if someday you end up dead in an alley, can I forget that, too? I can't, I just can't. I'm sorry. But I'll offer you this. I'll give you both the chance to tell your parents first. I think it'll go easier on you then. Tomorrow, I'll call. I hope by that time, they already know what's happened."

* * *

Katie and I met behind the tennis courts after school to discuss our predicament. What should we do? Mr. Lyme was a fucking asshole, that was for sure.

"Maybe it won't be so bad," Katie said. For her, it probably wouldn't be—her father didn't live at home and her mother didn't give a shit what she did. We smoked a joint. We also considered letting the air out of Joan's and Mr. Lyme's tires or maybe just running away. Finally we decided the longer we put it off the worse it would get, and headed slowly home.

At six o'clock my mother got home from Hofstra, where she worked as a secretary in the Public Safety office. She plopped herself down on our worn, flowered sofa and turned on the TV with the remote control. Slowly, I shuffled into the room behind her, pausing many times to go over what I was going to say. I slid onto the couch next to her, glancing over my clothes to see that there weren't any stray safety pins anywhere. I smoothed my hair, which I had just washed.

"Mom?" I said. "Mom?"

She turned her head and glared at me. "Shush! I'm in the middle of a show! Talk to me later. Or talk to your father when he gets home. I've had a long day. I don't want to talk to anyone under thirty for at least two hours."

She turned back to the flickering television, and I went upstairs. The phone rang, and I answered it after the first ring, thinking, Oh God, it's Mr. Lyme!

"Hi, ugly." It was only Katie. "I told my mother."

"So," I said, "What happened?"

"We argued for a while, you know, about drinking and drugs and the way I dress, and my grades, and how my father would have a fit. I said no way he'll ever know about anything that goes on with me, and I know she and

Dad used to smoke all kinds of shit in their room when they were together, and so on, and so on. I'm grounded for two weeks, but that won't last. Give it four or five days and she'll let me off. I'll do the dishes and vacuum for her, and she'll get all motherly, and we're sure to have a heart-to-heart talk and then I'll be ungrounded. How'd it go with you?"

I laughed, clenching my fist. "It didn't. She's watching TV, as usual, and doesn't want to hear from me. Screw it. I don't see why I should bother. I'm getting killed anyway, I might as well go with dignity. Look, I have to go, before my father comes home. I'll talk to you tomorrow, if I make it to school."

"Where are you—"

I hung up. It was the first time since I'd met Katie that I'd decided to do something completely on my own. But it wasn't fair that she got away with it when the shit was going to hit the fan in my house. I padded down the stairs, past my mother. Funny that I bothered to tiptoe—she wouldn't have noticed a grizzly bear passing through unless the television was showing reruns. I snuck out the back door, cutting through backyards for a few blocks, then popped back out onto the street and headed for Mike's.

When I got there I didn't say anything about what had happened because Mike had a bunch of his friends there for a barbecue in his backyard. I was a little annoyed because I wanted to be alone with him so he could calm me and make everything okay again. But I was relieved, too. Now I wouldn't have to explain things to Mike and face his anger. He *would* be angry, when I eventually told him, but it could wait. I'd just have a hamburger first.

The phone rang shrilly from the kitchen. Oh God, I thought again, it's Mr. Lyme! I tensed, but relaxed by the third ring. Consoling myself that the call couldn't be for me —probably no one even noticed I was missing yet—I bit into my burger and let juice drip over my chin.

"Mike!" called his mother from inside. "Is Nancy here? Her mother's on the phone. I told her I don't think she's here, but I didn't know for sure. Is she here?"

Mike started to answer, but I stopped him. "Tell her I'm not here!" I whispered. He looked at me like I was crazy. I *was* crazy. "Please," I said. He obeyed, then gripped my arm really hard, and dragged me into the driveway. I was slipping on the gravel. All Mike's friends were looking at me. Shit! Why did I have to be such a jerk! This wasn't the way to make a good impression. Shit.

"What's going on, Nancy?" Mike demanded.

I yanked my arm away from him. "Ouch!"

"What's going on?"

"You cooked this hamburger really well. It's not too red, not too burnt. Perfect."

"I'll ask again. What's going on?"

"Thanks for lying for me. I know how you hate to lie."

"Are you in trouble?"

"Jeez, your friends must think I'm such an asshole."

"Is your mother going to come down here, looking for you?"

Damn, that would really suck, wouldn't it? I was about to answer, when Mike's mother called to him again. "Mike, it's Mrs. Byer on the phone again. She wants to talk to you."

I shrugged. "Aren't you glad I didn't tell you anything yet? Now you don't have to lie when you say you have no idea what the hell's going on." Mike didn't find that funny, but went inside to the phone. Shit, I was in big fucking trouble.

He came back out a minute later, practically frothing at the mouth. And he didn't even know what happened at school yet! He was just pissed about my mother calling up and bugging him because I ran out without asking permission. But Mike was smart enough to know that something else was up, so I told him what happened. I was afraid he'd break my wrist if I didn't spit out the truth. Well, almost the truth. He couldn't even talk, he was so mad.

"Thanks for standing behind me!" I shouted, pulling my wrist free of his grip and running down the driveway. Then I kept running. Mike didn't follow, which really sucked. I was hoping he would, and we could make up and everything would turn out all right. Guess that was just another stupid fantasy of mine, that everything would somehow, someday, be all right.

I burrowed into a giant rhododendron on the front lawn of a nursing home at the end of Mike's block. Eventually he'd come after me, and he'd probably find me in here.

Two hours later, no one had come looking for me. I could even hear the stereo playing at Mike's, and pictured him guzzling beer and sucking down burgers, maybe dancing with some girl. What a shithead. Thinking about all the trouble I was in, I swore I'd never do anything bad again if I could just get out of it this once. Maybe, I thought, I should go stay with Katie. No way. Her mother hated me. Thought I was too much of a snob because I didn't go over to the house anymore and because I wasn't willing to sit and shoot the shit with her.

I lay down and looked up at the sky peeking through the leaves of the bush. I loved rhododendrons—they were like clubhouses, perfect for hiding out. Rolling onto my stomach, I noticed an empty beer bottle a few feet from my head. Without even thinking, I broke it against the trunk of the rhododendron, and sat up. Absently, I pressed the broken neck into my ankle and twisted it. My ankle started to bleed a little, and I dragged the dirty glass up my leg. I made a pretty bloody cross and stared at it. I was starting to cry and I couldn't stand it. I was such a jerk! Why couldn't I be a good, normal person? Why did I have to go and ruin things all the time? My parents would never forgive me, Katie would be mad that I hung up on her, Mike was probably already screwing someone else, and it was *all my fault*!

I lifted my shirt and punched my stomach with the broken glass. Pinpricks of blood oozed up on my belly, and I laughed bitterly through my tears. What did I think I was doing? Fixing things? If I was going to do it, I should do it right—slit my wrists and be done with it. But, of course, I didn't have the courage. I was just a big baby without enough courage for anything that was important. A big fucking wimp, screwing up everyone's life. Shit. Fuck. I threw the bottle out of the bush, dried my tears on my shirt, and crawled out of the bush. May as well go home and deal with the bullshit.

Chapter 10

I went home, and yeah, the shit hit the fan. Some parents might mellow if they thought there was a chance their daughter was gone for good, but not mine. Because I'd acted like a little kid, running away, I was told I'd be treated like a child. That meant a spanking—first with my mother's hand, for the drinking, which Katie's mother had called and told her about some time while I was in the rhododendron, then with a wooden spoon, for running, for "sleeping with who knows how many guys, fucking slut," and for not crying when I was spanked. I could cry at the drop of a pin, except when it might actually do me some good.

Finally, my father mentioned how worried Mike was—he'd been calling every half hour to see if I was home yet—and I started to cry. I got called some more choice names, got asked if I would turn tricks for a beer, got told I was not allowed to wear black or listen to P.I.L. or Billy Idol or The Clash or Bowie anymore.

I was grounded "indefinitely," and I slinked upstairs to call Mike. He apologized for before, said at least we'd see each other in school and said not to worry, in a week they'd mellow if I cut the shit. I didn't curse him out for leaving me to suffer under the bush for two and a half hours because I was so happy to at least have something left, even if it was only Mike. Katie called and luckily I picked up the phone before my mother could hang up on her. We talked for a while, and I almost felt better. Without changing into my pajamas, I went to bed.

The next morning I was almost late for school, which would have been bad since it turned out I had in-school suspension. Awesome! I thought when I heard. No classes! Katie and I passed notes between our desks whenever the teacher on duty in the suspension room wasn't looking, and wrote poems about drugs and getting wasted. We sneaked a joint in the bathroom at lunchtime. Then we snickered quietly and passed more notes all afternoon, and ogled a really gorgeous, long-haired known coke-head in the suspension room. What a life!

My mother was so mad at me, she refused to serve me dinner. She said that if I could afford to buy beer, I could afford to buy my own dinner. At first, I didn't mind much. I figured when I ran out of money, I could eat at Mike's or maybe at Katie's. Except, my mother informed me, I was still grounded, so I couldn't go out to anyone's house, even for a meal. After many arguments she finally conceded to let me eat food she'd bought, but only certain things, and I couldn't use the kitchen. The end result was un-buttered bread and cold SpaghettiOs, straight from the can.

After five days of that, I was willing to kiss my mother's feet if she'd serve me a real meal. Instead of acting self-righteous and angry, I started dusting and vacuuming and greeting her at the door with a sickeningly sweet smile every night. It worked. Soon I was off the top of her shit list, though I was still grounded—my father was in charge of that, and nothing would make him lift it before he was ready.

Of course, by the next weekend, school was out and Katie and I decided it wasn't fair for us to be grounded since we didn't really do anything wrong. We didn't even drink the beer we bought. Everyone was just trying to be pains in our asses. And so, Saturday night, we sneaked out of our houses and went to visit one of Katie's old friends.

"Andy, baby!" she cried, hugging his skinny, slumped figure. His hair was dirty-blond, and hung in long strings over his eyes. Looking at him, and the other guys around him, I was glad I was going out with such a straight-pin. Druggies, metal-heads, punkers—they're all the same. They all exist on weed, ups, sometimes acid or coke, junk food, and diet soda or beer. They all look like the sick puppies whose pictures are shown on cans next to 7-Eleven cash registers.

"Nancy," Katie said, pulling me into her embrace with Andy, "this is the boy who taught me to smoke my first joint! He taught me to French-inhale, hell, I think he even taught me to French *kiss*!" Andy blushed and smiled.

Next I met Andy's girlfriend and smoked a joint with her while Andy and Katie caught up on gossip. Sitting on the curb next to Cheri, the girlfriend, I tried to listen to them and not her. She was weird even for my tastes. Too open. Even under the influence of drugs, I kept my mouth shut among strangers, and this chick was sitting next to me on the curb telling me *everything*. Seemed she really loved Andy, and wanted to get married, but he said he wasn't ready.

"Why not wait awhile—he'll still be here," I said.

"Oh no," she corrected me, pulling at the knots in her dirty, brown hair, "Andy's got wandering eyes. Wait and see—pretty soon his dick will follow."

"Then he sucks," I said. "You don't need him."

She said again how much she loved him, and started

telling me what a great lay he was. I glanced at Katie, wishing she would come rescue me.

"I was on the pill for two years," Cheri went on, "but I haven't been taking it for almost a month, not since my last period. Andy doesn't know yet, but when he finds out I'm pregnant, he'll have to marry me." Cheri pushed herself off the curb and went to get that other joint. Good, I thought, because I need one. Not that Cheri and Andy weren't a great pair. They were both gross, and I could hardly believe Katie really cared about Andy. I was pretty sure she was putting on an act to get his weed.

We smoked some more and then went into Andy's house to use the bathroom and talk to his mother.

"Get me a beer!" Mrs. Corey said to Andy as soon as we were inside. "And who are all these people? What is this, a motel? A rest stop, maybe? You pay rent here? You ever do anything I ask? Who says you can come tromping through with your pot-head friends anytime you want?"

I was embarrassed, but Katie whispered that it was all an act, and scrunched into the couch next to Mrs. Corey, kissing her loudly.

"What, what do *you* want?" said the fat woman, wiping her cheek. "Thanks for visiting so often. Shit, I thought you were dead or something!"

"Hi, Ma. This is my best friend, Nancy."

"So? I should care?" She turned to me, her three chins wagging, and I smiled. I was uncomfortable and wished we would leave. The house was too small for us anyway. The small living room was almost completely filled by a dusty TV, knickknack shelf, couch, and Mrs. Corey's huge, terry-clothed body. Besides the living room there was a bathroom—decorated with broken tile, dirt, and cigarette ashes

—a cracked yellow kitchen, and two doors which I guessed led to Andy's and his mother's respective bedrooms.

Although it was a lot like Katie's home, at least hers didn't smell. And Katie's mother, however negligent, was polite. I didn't feel like I belonged in that dirty house with that smelly fat woman. But maybe I did. Mrs. Corey treated me the same as everyone else.

In one breath she yelled to Andy, "Where's my beer? Did you drink it?" And to me, "Sit down!" I obeyed, and she yelled for Andy to be a gentleman and bring his lady guests beers, too. She then launched into a speech about the evils of drugs, how they killed her husband and how we should be praying every day to the good Lord for help.

"And what is this?" she said, flicking at my safety pins. I shrank back into the sofa. "The two of you," she continued, meaning Katie and me, "are weird. I know about you. I know about this shit."

Andy laughed. "Give 'em a break, Ma! Come on, guys, let's get out of here, Ma wants to watch the tube alone. We got stuff to do."

We obediently said good-bye, and followed Andy through the kitchen to the door.

"Where you going?" his mother called from the couch.

"Out, Ma, just out."

"Get your ass back here! What do you mean, 'Just out'? That ain't an answer!"

"See ya, Ma!"

Andy threw a beer can at the screen door and everyone laughed.

We were out of weed, and Andy suggested that we buy some mescaline. I'd never tried it before, but Katie said it makes you laugh for something like eight hours and it's only three dollars a hit, so I said okay.

The weed had made me jumpy. We stuffed seven people into Andy's beat-up Ford, and besides worrying about getting caught buying mesc, I was stressed about Andy driving. I didn't like driving after smoking any more than driving after drinking, but Katie said it was okay because Andy was very careful, and a great driver.

Someone was blasting Pink Floyd's "Dark Side of the Moon" and the sound seemed to echo in my skull, to envelop me completely. It was frightening—I kept thinking we'd soon become headlines, like those kids you always read about in the paper. They were such good kids, their mothers say, they were too young to die.

We drove to Shore Road, the big drug place in Lindenhurst, and as we cruised slowly along the water, people slouched up to the car and asked what we were looking for. I was thinking, one of these guys will turn out to be a cop and we'll be screwed, but it didn't happen. Unfortunately, no one had any mesc either. We gave up and went to 7-Eleven to buy quart bottles of beer. After drinking some, I was much calmer and didn't think anything of it when Cheri suggested we go buy more weed. I forgot it was illegal.

Fifteen minutes later, we pulled in front of a Wyandanch deli and out of nowhere about fifteen men ran up to the car waving different-sized bags at our windows. Andy opened his a crack and slipped a five through it and, at the same time, one man pushed through a bag. As we pulled away from the curb, I was looking out the back window, watching the pushers slide off the trunk and run back to their buddies in the doorway of the deli. Suddenly I dropped my beer and gasped. "Cops!"

The car turned the corner behind us, flashing its lights.

Andy pushed the gas pedal to the floor and we took off. The cops followed. I yelled, "Please stop!" But no one listened.

"Whooee!" called Andy, screeching around a corner with only one hand on the steering wheel. I shut my eyes. The guy next to me was beating his hands on the back of the seat, singing, "I fought the law, and I won, we're fighting the law and we're gonna win . . ." Soon, all four guys were singing.

Katie, who was sitting in front of me, turned around and rolled her eyes. I couldn't even muster the humor to smile at her. I picked up my beer and distractedly gulped the last of it, wincing as the bottle clanked hard against my teeth when the car hit a bump.

I yelled again and this time Cheri chimed in. Worried about her kid, I guessed. We slowed and finally stopped. Then things got really weird. I wondered if I was stuck on a movie set.

One cop, a woman, shone her flashlight in my backseat window and I tried to cover the beer bottles with my feet. The other cop, a man, pulled Andy and the three guys on my left from the car.

"*Yo,* man!" said one of Andy's friends, pulling his denim jacket straight.

"Fuck you," said the cop.

"No, fuck *you,* pig," said another guy. "We have our rights."

The cop pushed him, hard. "No, *fuck you*! And quit the bullshit. Just give us the stuff, and no one gets hurt here tonight. Don't screw around, punk!"

Andy leaned back against the car and pulled a cigarette from his pocket. "What're you talkin' about, man?" he drawled.

The cop hit him in the face, banging his head once

against the door. "Don't *fuck* with me! Just give it up before I bust your head wide open, punk!"

"What'll happen to us?" I asked Katie.

She told me not to worry because they wouldn't even talk to us, they never bothered the girls. I wasn't so sure I believed her, but she turned out to be right. The guys eventually gave over the bag of weed. One cop dumped out the baggie in the dirt at the side of the road and scattered the weed with his foot. Then they let us go.

I asked to go home. My arm was bleeding from the cross I'd cut with my bottle cap under the glare of the flashlight.

Chapter 11

As summer progressed, I started getting caught for everything. The Fourth of July, Mike's parents were in Virginia visiting his grandparents. I wanted to go to a party he was throwing at his house and stay really late, which meant I had to sneak out. I didn't want Mike to know I was sneaking out, so to get away with it, I had to be at his house by ten o'clock. I told him not to bother picking me up because I had to eat dinner at my grandmother's house and I wasn't sure when I'd be home. At eight o'clock, I went upstairs, feigning sickness. At nine o'clock, I crept downstairs and out the front door while my parents were in the kitchen, arguing. It was raining out, so I didn't bring my purse. I hate when it gets wet because then everything inside gets wet too, and the cigarette butts in the bottom get gross and smell.

By nine-thirty I was at Mike's house being dried off. Since most of Mike's friends never went out until at least ten, the party was pretty dead. At around ten, everyone started showing up. Most of the people I recognized from my high school. I knew most of them weren't invited, but in a small town like Babylon you can't keep any party a secret. Mike's house would be trashed by midnight—already, people were lighting firecrackers in his kitchen sink. As I was pushing through the living room at about ten-thirty, looking for Katie and John, there was a knock on the front door. Since I was closest, I put down my drink—thank God—and answered it. Oh, hi Mom.

She grabbed me by the neck, and pulled me to the car. I yelled good-bye to Mike as he hurried outside after me, looking confused. Signaling that I'd explain later, I noticed he looked mad. Of course.

In the car, my mother said nothing at first. She stared straight ahead at the road, clutching the steering wheel, grinding her teeth. Then she started muttering terms of affection like "slut" and "tramp." We swerved into our driveway, spewing gravel. She grabbed me again by the hair, then yanked me up our front steps and into the living room, where my father was chain-smoking on the couch. My mother tossed me onto a chair and sat next to my father. It was beautiful how they became friends whenever I was in trouble.

There was silence for about twenty seconds, which seemed more like twenty minutes. Finally, my mother burst. "Have you had sexual intercourse with Michael Roman?" she practically screamed.

"No," I said, straight face and everything, "he doesn't like Chinese food." Of the hundreds of answers I could have chosen, I don't know why I picked that one. The term "brain-dead" comes to mind.

As my father tried to quiet his shaking hands and calmly pull another cigarette from the pack on the table, I noticed he was almost as red as its Marlboro trim. My mother reached for the ashtray. I was sure she intended to throw it at me. Instead, she only moved it closer, and lit a Virginia Slim. She then stood, very slowly, and carefully walked through the dining room into the kitchen. She returned with my army bag and threw it over the couch, over my father's head, and onto the coffee table, just missing the ashtray.

I winced. Without looking at my mother or me, my father reached forward and turned the bag upside down. I thought, they must've spent a half hour choreographing this whole scene before Mom came to get me. But even so, oh boy, my life was flashing before my eyes in that instant before everything toppled onto the table.

Out came sticks of black eyeliner, safety pins and paper clips, scraps of paper, carefully folded notes from Katie. That stuff was okay, so long as they didn't read Katie's notes. The other stuff was plenty to put me away for a few months. Six or seven old cigarette boxes. God, I thought, I hope they didn't look inside them and discover the roaches. I should've put them somewhere else. But the cigarette boxes were not the biggie there. They were overshadowed by the pretty, round, birth-control-pill case sitting on top of the heap. I didn't say anything—I figured it was up to them. I was busy cursing myself for being so stupid. If only I hadn't gone to the party. If only I'd waited until they were in bed before sneaking out. If only I didn't leave my purse at home. If only I kept my pills under my mattress or something. Shit.

"Mrs. Harris called to see if you could baby-sit tomorrow night. I checked upstairs to see if you were still awake," said my mother. "Imagine my surprise—my fright—when I discovered your bed empty!"

My father pressed out his cigarette. "We looked in your purse because we were worried. We wanted some clue to where you were." He picked up the pills. "And here it was. Clue, evidence, everything." He got up to make himself a drink.

"How could you do this to us?" said my mother.

"Do this to you? I didn't do anything to you! Why do you take everything as a personal offense to you? Why do you think everything I do has something to do with you?"

"First the drinking, now this," she went on. "Do you have any idea what you're putting your father and me through? Do you know what you're doing to us?"

"Mike and I are in love. I'm old enough to make my own decisions."

My father sat down, and my mother took his glass, drinking half of its contents before continuing. "You make me sick! Who the hell do you think you are?"

"You know, you think Amy Brown and Keely Simpson and Joan Ferrow are so great, but they're not virgins either!"

"If we had any sense, we'd throw you the hell out!" my mother yelled, sweeping most of the contents from my purse onto the floor with her arm.

"In fact, I was probably the last person in the whole school to get laid!"

My father raised his eyebrows. "Don't you use that language in my house, young lady."

"Look at what you wear!" my mother yelled. "You can't even dress right, and I'm supposed to believe you're old enough to sleep with Michael? I'm supposed to believe you know what *love* is?"

"We're getting married eventually, anyway. What's the difference if we're having sex now, or later?"

"The difference? The *difference*?" My mother shook her head as though she couldn't understand what I was saying.

"Why can't you leave me alone? Why can't you accept that I'm a big girl now? It's not fair."

"You live in this house, you do as we say," my father said, pointing his finger at me.

"It isn't fair for you to treat me like a baby. I'm old enough to know what I want," I said as I reached for the pill package.

My father slapped my hand and yelled, "What happens if you get pregnant?"

"You never listen to me. Stop playing almighty pure—I bet you did the same thing when you were my age!"

"The pill isn't one hundred percent infallible, you know, Little Miss Smart-Ass."

"And I bet *you* weren't in love! I'm in love! There's nothing wrong with sex if you're in love, is there?"

My mother jumped in on the pregnancy spiel then, arguing, "What happens to your life if you get pregnant now? You can't get an abortion. Your father and I wouldn't sign the papers. You'd have to drop out of school and take care of your child."

"We don't do it that often, anyway. Why can't you just accept it? You can't change what's already happened."

"I hope if you ever have a child, it grows up to be just like you."

"Normal parents aren't like this. They support their children."

"Normal children aren't like this," said my father, patting down the tuft of hair he tried to keep over his bald spot. "You're not allowed to see Mike anymore."

"Bull*shit*! Uh uh, no way. You can ground me, maybe, even though it isn't fair, but you can't make me stop seeing him. I'll just sneak around more if you do that!"

"I don't think he's good for you. You're too young for him. You should go out with someone your own age."

"Guys my age screw around too, you know! Forget it, I'm not going to stop seeing him."

I stomped upstairs, but I had to sneak down once to call

Mike, so I could explain what happened. He was too upset to be angry, though he called me stupid for leaving my pills in my bag and sneaking out to his party. I didn't care what he thought of me, as long as he forgave me, which he did.

Lying on my bed and absently brushing a piece of glass back and forth across my arm, I started thinking that I was tired of crying. I was tired of everything. I hated my house, I couldn't wait to leave. Maybe if I got a good job, I could move out. I wouldn't even say good-bye, I'd just pack my stuff and disappear while Mom and Dad were at work one day.

I tiptoed downstairs, pulled the newspaper off the coffee table and brought it back to my room. After reading "Ann Landers" and "Joyce Brothers," and tearing off the front page so I'd always remember the night my parents drove me crazy—"*Newsday*, July 4th, 1986," I flipped through to the classifieds and combed through "Apartments for Rent." Three hundred a month for a studio apartment in Babylon —probably a rat hole, but I could live in it. With electricity and stuff, I could probably live on something like four hundred a month. But how would I pay for college? Well, I wouldn't have to go.

Imagine! I could set up a bar, and everyday I could learn to make a new kind of drink. Katie could come over and taste what I made. We wouldn't have to drink a lot, we'd just try stuff. I always wanted to be a bartender—what a great way to learn! At Christmas, we could throw a big party and everyone who came would have to bring a decoration for the tree. Wow! It would be so cool!

Oh, who am I kidding? I thought, it'll never happen. I'd never have the fucking *guts* to do it! I opened my night table drawer and pushed through tissues, cassettes, per-

fume bottles, and broken pencils until I found a jagged
piece of glass from the vase that used to be on my desk.

I looked at my arms and laughed through my sobs. So
many scars! I looked like I'd been through a meat grinder.
Christ, I hardly knew where to cut—there was so little
space left. It must have been like a heroin junky, always
searching for a vein that's not too hard. Right above the
crook of my elbow looked pretty clear. But I'd go over that
cross a little. I wondered if I'd bleed, cutting on top of a
scar. Only one way to find out.

I started by carefully going over some of the older scars—
concentration made me feel better—but soon my mind
wandered. I started thinking about the mess I was in. Even
if I managed to sneak out and see Mike, it would be impossible to be alone together.

It's over now, I thought. There's no hope. I don't know
why I even want to bother living anymore. Shit, this sucks.
This really sucks. I grew more reckless with the glass. I
wasn't even looking at my arm, so it was a few minutes
before I noticed what I'd done. Scratches from forearm to
wrist, crisscrossing, cutting straight lines, crooked lines,
oozing small drops of blood everywhere. Pretty.

Chapter 12

By July eighth, the day before my sixteenth birth-day, I was still grounded. Besides the fact that I wanted to celebrate my birthday with Katie and Mike, I hoped I'd get out soon because it was about ninety fucking degrees in the house. Since I cut up my arm, I had to wear long-sleeved shirts all the time. Mostly, I lay on my bed with a wet washcloth on my forehead.

Just about the time I was sure I'd die of boredom if the heat didn't get me first, my mother called upstairs to say Katie was on the phone. I knew things must be getting better if I was allowed to take phone calls.

"So, how's the almost-birthday girl?" asked Katie.

"Still grounded," I answered, "But I should be out soon." I really wanted to light a cigarette, but I knew if I smoked in the house I'd be grounded forever.

Katie chuckled. "I should be so lucky. You know my mother let me off for the drinking, right? So last night I went out with Andy and Cheri and some other people I don't really like. Too bad you weren't there. We totally tripped on mesc for like four hours, and then one of Andy's friends took out a vial of cocaine and started doing lines, so I tried that."

"Katie!"

"What? What's the big deal?"

I snorted loudly, pretending to be offended. "I thought

we weren't going to try anything new unless we were to-gether?"

Katie laughed. "Don't worry, you didn't miss much. I mean, it was a good high but my nose has never hurt so much. It was a hundred times worse than sniffing Tylenol. But anyway, let me finish my story before my mother gets home and takes the phone away from me. Okay, so I got home at three in the morning, figuring my mother would be asleep in bed with some guy, but there she was, waiting for me when I got in!"

I rolled my eyes. "Uh-oh, Katie, I don't think I want to hear this . . ."

"Shh, let me finish," Katie continued. "So my mother goes, 'Young lady, do you know what time it is?'

"I tried to look at my watch, but my arm got all twisted up so it was upside down. 'I dunno, nine-thirty?' I ended up saying.

"My mother jumped up like a jack-in-the-box then and said something like, 'Don't play games, little miss. Where the fuck were you until three in the morning?'

"I thought she was joking because you know she never pays attention to when I come in. Plus I felt really sick. And *really* beat, I mean it was three in the morning! I wanted to go to bed! I said to my mother, 'Well, Ma, I was sittin' in this gay bar, naked, doin' lines, an' sudd'nly the guy nexta me said, "Hey, wanna free base?" An' I said, "What the hell?"'

"At this point, Nancy, my eyes were shutting. I must've looked pathetic. My mother slapped me and I fell down, but I was so happy not to be standing up anymore I didn't mind being hit. Then I argued with myself on the floor for a little while. I turned my head one way and said, 'You're wasted,' then I turned it the other way and said in a deeper voice, 'No I'm not.' 'Yes you are,' 'No I'm not,' and so on until my mother kicked me in the ribs and sent me to my room.

"Then I'm not sure exactly what happened, but I ended up in the kitchen with my head in the oven, the gas turned on, and vomit on the front of my shirt. Now my mom thinks I'm suicidal and feels guilty as shit. Uh-oh, speaking of the bitch, I hear her coming in now. Gotta run, Nan! Call you tomorrow!" Click.

I was confused and felt like I really needed to talk to Katie for at least another half hour to get her story straight, but I was glad she was okay.

"Nancy?" said my mother, coming into the room behind me as I stared at the phone.

I jumped, and then slowly turned to face my mother, afraid she might have been listening in on the phone conversation on the downstairs phone.

My mother sat on the couch and picked at the hem of her skirt. "I just wanted to say that your father and I feel you've learned your lesson about sneaking out of the house. We still intend to have a long talk with you about the birth control pills, but since tomorrow's your birthday, we're going to lift your grounding." Having said that, she quickly got up and left. I was a little stunned and very much overjoyed. I picked up the phone and almost called Katie, but decided to wait until later when her mother would probably be out. Instead, I called Mike and made plans for the evening.

Chapter 13

Since the next day was my birthday, Katie talked her mother into freeing her for the day. We of course went out to celebrate.

Katie had a pipe of hash, which I'd never smoked before. She said after doing hash, you never want to go back to plain weed. She was right.

We went to the Sunrise Mall and smoked outside, near the broken, rusty bike racks next to the bus stop. It was even hotter than the day before. We both wore black tank tops rolled up and tucked into our bras, just like we did when we first met almost a year earlier and sat behind the school tennis courts smoking a joint.

We only smoked one pipeful of the hash, but before we even finished that much, we were choking with laughter. As I gasped for air, I realized I didn't even know what I was laughing at. Skipping into the mall, we tried to keep straight faces. But it was so bad, we couldn't even look at each other because then we were afraid we'd fall on the floor or something, we'd be laughing so hard. In a way it kind of sucked because we were going to steal some clothes and jewelry, but we were too conspicuous with those joker-grins on our faces.

Katie started coming down before I did. She didn't come down hard, like when we crashed after the Christmas Trees, so it was cool. She made fun of me because she was straight while I was still blown off my ass. I could feel a big wide grin stretched across my face, and I couldn't make it go away. I tried pulling the corners of my mouth down but Katie laughed as my smile pushed back up.

"What's so damn hilarious?" I demanded between giggles.

"Forget it," said Katie, "Forget trying not to look silly. It makes you look even dumber. You look like a clown! You look like a—"

"Now just wait a second," I interrupted, "I look okay to me." Walking very erect, I approached a stringy-haired sixties-throwback sitting near us on a bench. "Excuse me," I asked her, "how do I look to you?"

"Stoned," she said, looking away.

I started laughing so hard, you'd think I'd never heard anything so funny in my life. Katie was shushing me, but she was still laughing almost as much as me.

A good half hour later, I finally regained control of myself. I was somber and exhausted, and so was Katie. We got on the first N19 bus we saw. At least we thought it said N19, though we weren't absolutely sure.

We told each other stupid jokes for a while and soon twenty minutes had passed, but we still weren't home. We weren't even close it seemed, since neither of us recognized anything we saw outside. Katie swaggered to the front of the bus and said, "Excuse me, can you tell me when we're getting to Babylon?"

"Babylon? Girl, this bus don't *ever* get to Babylon!"

"Oh. Can you let us off at the next stop then?"

We got off the bus, no idea where we were, and we were *laughing*. Maybe the hash hadn't completely worn off after all. We should've been worried since neither of us had any money. But we knew that as a last-ditch effort, we could always call Mike or John, collect. We decided to try hitching first.

Katie stuck out her thumb—somehow she got rides much faster than me. When a car whizzed by, we cursed it, giving our middle fingers plenty of exercise. Finally, a truck stopped about fifty feet from us. We ran to it, and the scummy-looking, hadn't-washed-in-a-week driver told us to jump in back and hold on. I was barely in when he screeched away from the curb, and I nearly fell out.

The truck was partly filled with pipes and planks of wood and other junky looking stuff which rolled and slid, making an awful lot of noise. I was starting to feel miserable. Up front, only about twenty feet from us since the truck was small, sat the driver and another guy. Katie and I stepped over the debris, toward them, though I was reluctant—the possibility of something bad happening was stuck in my mind. I wanted the option of jumping out the back. The guy in the passenger seat turned around, reached into a bag sitting between him and his friend, and offered Katie and me beers. We turned them down. Then the driver lit a joint, offered it, and Katie took a hit. I accepted it from her, though I was nervous as hell. Suddenly, I noticed we weren't going down the main road anymore, but had turned down a street which led toward the water.

"This isn't the right way," I said.

The driver slowly turned his head. "Don't sweat it. We have to go by a house down here, where we did some work. We just have to drop off a key."

"I'm in a hurry to get home. Maybe you should just let us off here."

The passenger touched Katie's arm and she jerked it back. "What's up with your friend? What's she worried about?" he asked.

"Ups," said Katie. "She's just coming down." I nodded and smiled shakily.

"We'll just drop off the key," said the driver, pulling in front of a white-shingled house, "and then we'll get you girls home. No sweat."

I was scared shitless. Please God, let it be okay, I prayed. Please let them just bring us home now. I won't ever hitch again. I really won't, I know it's not safe, I know that now, please don't let them hurt us.

I began to think, as I sat watching reruns of *Cheers* and *L.A. Law* that night, that maybe my luck would simply never run out. The men did finally drive us home. We asked them to drop us off in front of a store a few blocks away from my house, so no one from our families would see us. Katie walked me the rest of the way home, and all the while I'd forgotten about thanking God for getting us home safe.

Chapter 14

Nothing much happened the rest of that summer. Neither Katie nor I was grounded again. We were both extra careful. Mike the jerk told his mother all about why I was grounded. She didn't let me go to his house for a while, but since she was at work all day it didn't much matter what her orders were. At night, since it was summer, Mike and I mostly hung out in the backseat of his car.

I was happy when school started again because it meant I could see Katie every day. In fact, now that Mike and John were both in college, I could spend every lunch period with her. We still intended to see a lot of our boyfriends on the weekends, since Mike was only a half hour away and John was about an hour.

That September was my sophomore year. I thought it would be just like the year before, only better and more fun, but I discovered that it might be much more difficult. I walked into social studies class eighth period and discovered that we had a new teacher. She took one look at my torn sandals, bleach-splotched jeans, and safety-pinned tank top and decided I was trouble. After class, she called me to her desk and curtly explained to me how she ran her classroom. As she spoke, it dawned on me that I no longer had a good reputation to hide behind. My grades were barely average, and I'd been suspended once.

But Katie's and my habits didn't change very much. We

still went to the Chinese restaurant for lunch most of the time and we still got high almost every day. We didn't take ups anymore because the girl who used to sell them to us had graduated.

I was tired of rarely having any money, and I'd grown to hate baby-sitting. Kids were such brats. Katie got a job in Shop Rite, and I knew it wasn't fair for her to pay my way all the time. Unlike Mike, she wasn't getting anything out of being my benefactor. So I started looking for a job. I wished a job would just fall into my lap, so I wouldn't have to walk around town asking everyone, "Do you need help?" I got desperate, and began pounding the pavement, as they say.

Finally, I started working in a print shop. It was dull—I folded and collated—but it was still money. The only thing I really hated to do was use the stitching machine. It was a big, old piece of equipment which acted as a giant stapler, for fastening books of paper up to an inch or two thick. Very powerful. First, a metal bar pounded down on the stack of paper, flattening it, then the machine wrapped wire through it. Then the wire got cut underneath, making staples. It made an awful noise when it was operated and every time I had to use it I was warned to watch out for my fingers. While I worked, my morbid mind imagined what it would be like to get my finger stuck in the machine. Yuck! Thinking about it sent chills down my spine. I guessed that was good, because it made me more careful.

The best part about the print shop was that I was making about sixty dollars a week. That gave me more money for drugs and food when I got the munchies.

Because I was afraid that I'd lose Mike if all the extra potato chips and donuts began to show around my waist, I began vomiting after dinner at home. Sticking a finger down my throat was too gross, so I used the end of my toothbrush.

The funny thing about my money was that I still couldn't buy that much stuff, because my parents only let me keep twenty-five dollars a week for myself. The rest went into the bank. About twenty dollars went for drugs and munchies, which left me with five dollars, just enough for cigarettes. It was a good thing I knew how to shoplift.

The way Katie and I stole clothes from big department stores was by wearing old clothes we no longer wanted under our other outfits when we went shopping. We went into the dressing room with whatever we wanted to steal, took off the tags and switched them with our old clothes. We left the dressing room with the same number of items we brought in and no one suspected a thing. Just to be safe, we never gave the dressing-room girl the clothes. We always said we were going to take them, and put them out on the racks ourselves.

The one time we almost got caught, I gave Katie my old clothes to hang on the racks for me. She thought one of the blouses really belonged to the store, so instead of returning it to a rack right away, she asked a girl at the register where it belonged. The girl didn't know, but called her supervisor to help Katie find the right rack. I came out of the dressing room, and saw Katie with an older woman, who was searching through the blouse for tags. I flipped! I wanted to run right out of the store, but I couldn't leave Katie alone, so I went and stood by her.

Luckily, the woman only looked confused, said, "I'm not sure *where* this goes—for some reason it hasn't any tags— I'll find a place for it later. Thank you, girls." As soon as she turned away, I practically sprinted from the store.

"Are you out of your fucking *mind*?" I asked Katie outside. She didn't know what I was talking about, so I explained. She turned red, embarrassed by her stupidity, then laughed because once again we had gotten away with it, like we got away with almost everything. After that, we went to a shoe store and while Katie flirted with the young manager, I stuffed two pairs of sandals into my army bag and walked out. We went to another shoe store and Katie left her shoes outside, walked in barefoot, put on a pair of shoes and walked out. People could be so dumb. I still don't know how we got away with it all.

The day before Thanksgiving, school was off, so Katie and I went to the mall. We loafed around a head shop–jewelry store for a while, pointing out all the drug paraphernalia we couldn't afford to buy, when I spotted a plastic showcase for earclips. Pointing to one, I asked Katie, "Isn't this one nice?" Next second, it was off the cardboard and in my pocket. I'd never done that before—just stuffed something in my pocket without some sort of premeditated plan. To keep up appearances, I didn't run out of the store right away. I browsed for another ten minutes, picked out and purchased a pair of earrings, and then left. Piece of cake.

The only problem with stealing from stores in the mall instead of the department stores closer to home was that except for Macy's, everything was too small to get away with our regular clothing scam. But we couldn't leave without stealing at least one item of clothing. We waited until almost closing time when everyone was busy, and Katie brushed into a rack of shirts sitting at the edge of a small Indian clothing store. Suddenly a tank top was stuffed under her blouse and she was walking away.

It wasn't too smart, because everyone who saw her knew what was going on, and I noticed the girl at the counter picking up the phone. I grabbed Katie's arm and we ran into Macy's, to the restroom. Katie ripped off the shirt's tag, took off her T-shirt and put the stolen tank on underneath. She put her own shirt back on inside out, so it looked a little different. We were both wearing black lipstick and had our hair spiked, which was too easy a description to track. We wiped our lips clean and flattened our hair with water.

Finally we left the restroom and quickly got to the bus stop, trying hard not to look nervously over our shoulders. Maybe, I thought, it's time we stop this. Like everything else, we were getting careless, and it wouldn't be long before we got caught.

Chapter 15

November, December, January, February—the months passed quickly and I hardly noticed them. Katie and I spent nearly every day stoned, high, tripping, or drunk. Somehow I still managed to get work done for school, but my grades were slipping. But I didn't get caught doing anything wrong, so my parents didn't catch on. During those winter months life grew progressively more dull. The only thing which still held my fascination was cutting. Even when I was happy, I sometimes looked at my scars, and thought about making new ones. I used cutting to celebrate my happiness as much as to ease my hurt.

By spring, my arms were crisscrossed with brown scabs, pink and white scars, and fresh red cuts. That was another thing about winter—no one ever saw the cuts beneath my clothes. I was inspired to cut more than usual.

Although I hated winter, I somewhat dreaded spring because it would mean I'd eventually have to bare my arms to the world again. I preferred to keep them to myself, so I could stare at the awesome destruction and mutilation I'd done all by myself. Still, I couldn't stop Mother Nature, and before I knew it, the crocuses were blooming in my front lawn.

Katie went to Florida with her mother over Easter vacation. I was really glad I was working at the print shop, because although Mike was off from school too, he had to work every day. I'd have been awfully lonely if it weren't for my job.

The day before we had to go back to school, Katie called me. I didn't have to work, so I was especially happy to hear from her.

"How was Disney World?" I asked.

"It was great," she said, "except for being with my mother. Of course she drove me crazy—she didn't want to *do* anything. She only wanted to sit by the hotel pool and flirt with young guys. And they really did hang around the old hag, too! I think maybe she was buying their drinks or something. But anyway, I have the *best* surprise for you! You *have* to come out today, it's real nice out, it's our last day of vacation, and I'm throwing a party. Only you and me are invited. It doesn't feel like we've talked for a long time, and I've been thinking a lot lately. There's a lot I have to say, and you're the only one I can say it to. Besides, I *happen* to have two sixes of beer, a pint of vodka, and a pint of Scotch to make our day more merry."

I was happy. I was finally going to get my vacation, even if it had to be crammed all into one day. "Where'd you get it all?" I asked.

Katie laughed her best I'm-so-smart-sometimes, and-the-rest-of-the-world-is-so-dumb laugh. "The hotel liquor cabinet was fully stocked," she said, "and my mother had a key. I took it upon myself to borrow it. Actually, I almost didn't get away with it. Of course, I couldn't steal anything early in the trip, because then she'd see that stuff was missing. So I waited until yesterday and just as my mother was stepping into the elevator, I said, 'Wait, I forgot something.' I ran with the set of keys back to the room and threw the booze into my duffel bag. Oh shit, I hear the witch coming.

Meet me by the lake in half an hour, okay? Oh, and wait until you see what I did to my hair. You're gonna love it. I know John will. Well, fuck him, anyway. I can do what I want with my life." She hung up.

I was confused. What was she talking about? Katie always said she'd *never*, not in a million *years*, do *anything* to her hair. Her hair? Maybe she colored it? Every time I touched up the black in my hair when the roots began to show, Katie would warn that I'd be bald by the time I was forty. Then she'd tilt her head forward and shake thick blond hair in my face. It didn't seem likely she'd ever do more than spike the top of her hair, and she definitely wouldn't color it.

I grabbed my army bag, left a note for my parents, who were at their friends' house for a party, and walked toward Argyle Park.

I saw Katie sitting on a green wooden bench by the side of the lake, a big red duffel bag on the ground beneath her feet. I ran up the grassy hill, and sat down next to her.

"What's with the scarf?" I asked, gesturing to the red-and-white bandanna tied tightly around her head.

She didn't answer, but handed me a beer, and in unison, we chugged. Then she took our empty cans, threw them across the lawn, and, still silent, handed me a small bottle of vodka. She held the Scotch. Something was wrong, and I hated not knowing what it was. Katie leaned her head back and tilted the bottle at her lips. At the same time, her other hand pulled off the scarf.

Oh my God, oh my God, oh my God. She'd shaved her head. All Katie's beautiful hair, her favorite part of her body, she'd shaved off.

"I know," she whispered, looking at me as a tear slid over

her cheek. "I'm an idiot. But the cutting didn't seem like enough. I had to *do* something. I had to show everyone they can't push me around and get away with it. John had to learn."

I gulped air as though I was drowning. Holy shit, I thought, at least she's not dead. Her hair will grow back. Thank God she's not dead. "What did John say when he saw it?"

"He hasn't seen anything yet, but he will. I talked to him on the phone. I *said* I would do it. He probably wasn't listening, as usual. From now on, he'll listen. Oh boy, will he ever!" Katie gulped a little more Scotch, grimaced as she swallowed, and capped the bottle. I started to cap my bottle too, but she stopped me. "No, you keep drinking. This is your party, remember?"

"Yours, too," I said.

"Mostly yours. Drink!"

So I did, finishing the vodka in thirty minutes. When I was about three quarters of the way through, I felt my face getting numb, and I thought, I'm drunk now, why don't I just stop? But then I looked at the inch or so left in the bottle, and decided, I've come this far, may as well finish it. Funny. It reminded me of the assembly we had in school where some people showed a movie about alcoholism and passed around question sheets. Supposedly, if you answered more than six questions with yes, you were an alcoholic. One question was, "Do you feel you always have to drink until the bottle is empty?"

"Let's go for a walk," Katie said.

I agreed because I figured I probably needed to walk off some of the vodka. Besides, I needed cigarettes.

Katie and I walked around the lake and cut through the

baseball field toward the center of town. We left her duffel bag at the park because if anyone wanted to steal what was left of the alcohol, we figured it wouldn't matter because we'd had enough.

As we approached the school's football field on the other side of the lake, Katie suddenly started laughing. Then she started to cry, and finally to talk.

"I got home at three o'clock yesterday, and I went to John's house to surprise him because I hadn't seen him for a week. Shawna Field was there. He said it was nothing, he was only helping her with her math, but I don't know. I made him make her leave and he was really mad. He said we're not married, and that he wants to see other people. I said 'you bastard,' and he slapped me and I stormed out. I shaved my head when I got home. I wasn't ever going to talk to him again, but I love him and he says he loves me, so this morning I called and apologized. I'm such a wimp, Nancy. How can you be friends with me when I'm such a wimp? No wonder he doesn't respect me! But I guess it's true, we're not married and I have no right to tie him down. I don't want to lose him, but I don't know what to do because I don't want him fucking Shawna the slut!"

I stopped walking. My head was spinning—I wished Katie hadn't let me drink so much. I'd have been much more help to her sober. As it was, I could barely comprehend her words. It seemed like I was standing still on the dirt path for an hour, staring at Katie's shiny head and swaying while I tried to think of something to say.

Katie laughed. "I know you're drunk. It's okay, it's my fault. Everything's my fault."

"No," I said slowly. "No it's not. You tell John it's not okay for him to screw around. You tell him I said it's not okay 'cause you're my best friend and you deserve better than that! If he can't love you right, he better leave you alone. Fuck him. You do so much for him, the least he could do is do so much for you." We were walking again, back toward our stuff. Katie had her arm around mine as we passed through the playground again, but I could hardly feel her touch. I looked at her and she was all blurry, but I kept talking about what an asshole John was. I knew I must be really drunk, but I'd be okay soon, as long as I kept walking and talking. I'd better be okay, because I had to be sober by four o'clock.

"You've been good to him," I said, "And now he has to be good to you because that's fair and if he isn't fair, he should be thrown out of ev'rythin', you know?"

Katie smiled. "Mellow, Nancy, everything'll be cool, I just needed to talk. Nancy?"

I fell forward onto the grass.

The next day I woke up at two o'clock and I didn't remember anything. It was really scary. No one was home—they were all at work or school, so I had to wait until three o'clock to find out what happened. I didn't even know if I was in trouble with my parents, or what. I did remember my mother at one point pushing me toward the bathroom, mumbling something about first time you get really drunk. I remembered I was going to say something, but I hadn't.

I spent half the day in the bathroom, feeling sick, and the other half at the phone wondering if I should call Katie at school. Every time I decided to call, I'd feel sick and rush back to the bathroom. Finally, by two-thirty, I began to feel better.

At three o'clock I called Katie, and as she told me all that happened, bits and pieces returned to my memory. Shit, I couldn't believe I passed out like that. I couldn't believe I didn't remember anything. Weird. She said yesterday, after drinking the vodka and going to buy cigarettes, I was walking next to her, talking, and suddenly I wasn't making sense anymore. Then I fell forward onto my face. She didn't know what to do, so she picked me up and I giggled.

Katie laughed into the phone. "So then I asked if you could stand and you said yes, but when I let go, you collapsed again! Don't you remember?"

I said I could just barely remember falling down and thinking how neat it was that I could fall so hard without feeling a thing. I remembered seeing green.

"Lucky for us," Katie continued, "Paul was walking through the park. Remember Paul? My friend from grade school who's a nerd at Chaminade prep school now? Well, he helped me carry you back to where our stuff was."

I pulled my terry cloth robe tighter and bit my nails. I could vaguely remember seeing Paul.

"You were squirming a lot, and at one point you wiggled free, landing flat on your back on the concrete. Before Paul and I could catch you, you'd crawled under a bush." Katie laughed. "Then you said you wanted to sleep there, under the bush. Doesn't any of this sound familiar?"

"Yeah," I lied.

"Okay, so we pulled you out of the bush and tried to make you sit, but you fell off the bench. Paul had some Doritos which I thought would make you throw up, so we fed them to you. You couldn't even chew. I had to move your mouth up and down, and even then you couldn't swallow. Doritos oozed out the sides of your mouth and onto your chin. It was gross, girl. You're lucky I'm still your friend. You couldn't even hold a cigarette in your mouth. Now, are you ready for this?"

I nodded, though I knew Katie couldn't see me.

"I had to put my finger down your throat," Katie went on, "until you vomited up some of the alcohol. Gross! You *owe* me!"

There was a long pause on the phone line. "Come on," I said, "what happened then? How'd I get home?"

Katie paused a second longer before speaking. "Sorry. I was lighting a cigarette. Okay, so at about four in the afternoon, Paul and I kind of half walked, half dragged you home. Your parents weren't there, so we carried you upstairs and threw you in bed. I left a note for your mother saying you ate something bad. And speaking of something bad, my mother'll be home soon, and I'm supposed to have a meatloaf in the oven. I have to go mix it up. Call me later. 'Bye!"

I hung up, wondering how much trouble I'd be in with my parents when they got home. Maybe they believed the note about me eating something bad, or maybe they'd figured I'd suffered enough. For once they'd be right. I remembered how last night I woke up sure I was going to die. Oh God, I'd wished, if you get me through this, I'll never drink again. Holy shit, my head had felt like it was stuck in a vise grip and was being slowly squeezed until it was going to explode. I couldn't even open my mouth, it felt stuffed with thick, dry cotton. Okay, maybe I'd drink again, but not that much.

Katie said she went to John's house after taking me home. The head shaving worked, because he cried and apologized and everything was hunky-dory again. I hoped he'd stop hurting her now. I wondered if Katie and I would ever live normal-people lives. I wondered if my father was going to kick my ass when he got home, or if he'd just make himself a drink and ignore me. I hoped for that. I didn't want to discuss my stupidity. I didn't even think I'd tell Mike, because I knew he'd be mad and I didn't feel up to fighting.

Chapter 16

Spring seemed to make everything work out. My parents never said anything about my Argyle Park experience, and John and Katie were back together and having a good time. A couple of weeks after Easter break, they were back to having sex every other night, and Katie and I were back to getting stoned every other day.

One beautiful sunny day in April, Katie and I cut out of social studies eighth period to get high. Usually I was very careful about using drugs or drinking before work, but this time, although I only took about four hits, I was definitely not straight. Since I wasn't totally obliterated, I figured it didn't matter. I'd probably only be folding papers. Maybe I'd get a paper cut.

When I got to work though, I discovered that I was supposed to staple packets of raffle tickets with the stitching machine. I admit I was a little startled when my boss gave his instructions to me, but I wasn't worried. I felt okay, even if I was a little spaced-out. I figured I'd just go slow, and be careful.

The good thing about the job was that once I got started on something it became automatic and I no longer had to think. I could daydream about Mike, or whatever I wanted. Still, I shouldn't have let my mind wander at the stitching machine, no matter how mindless the work was. I should've concentrated on what I was doing. Pick up collated raffle book. Jog the pages so the edge is flat. Slide under stitching machine guard. Press foot pedal. *Kachung!*

It was very hot in the print shop because there weren't any windows. Plus the pot I'd smoked made me a little woozy. Instead of concentrating on my work, I started thinking about other things. I was thinking about seeing Mike that night, since it was Friday. I wondered if I really did love him. Although questioning myself upset me, sometimes I wasn't sure I was really in love. I also wondered if he loved me. Probably more than I do him, I thought, mindlessly putting books into the machine and stapling them. I mean, look at all the money he spends on me. Tonight we may even go out to dinner.

I got a new box of collated books to staple, then resumed daydreaming. Hmmm, I thought, what will I wear? I don't have anything really pretty and appropriate.

It was so hard to dress for going out with Mike, especially when we were really going *out,* not just to his house to watch a video. I wanted to look pretty, but I had to keep my outfit simple so it could be easily removed. Belts and too-big jewelry were out of the question, as were any shirts or pants that I'd have to pin for any reason. A pin could open, and Mike would be angry about being pricked in the throes of passion. Besides, he would get frustrated trying to undress me, if it were too difficult. Patience was not his strongest point.

I was really moving fast with my stapling. I was going so quickly, I didn't bother to remove my foot from the pedal each time I completed a book. My boss came to the back of the shop and told me to slow down, be careful; and yet there I was, working very fast and not taking my foot off the pedal. And for some reason, when a book got stuck, I left my foot there on the pedal while I reached my finger beneath the guard to free the paper from where it was caught. I wasn't thinking; my foot moved automatically. *Kachung!* Holy shit, I thought, using my other hand to take my left finger, and the raffle book to which it was stapled, from the machine. I walked quickly to the front of the shop. "Hey," I said.

My boss looked up from the press. I was smiling, because it was kind of ironic that I should get hurt right after being warned to be careful. Besides, it didn't hurt much, though it looked pretty gross.

"Guess what? I got my finger caught in the thing back there!"

Everything went crazy. My boss and his assistant dropped what they were doing and ran to me, my boss shouting to his receptionist to call an ambulance. As the two men reached me, I tried to tell them I didn't need an ambulance, it wasn't that bad, it didn't hurt much. Probably a Band-Aid would do the trick.

"Just don't move," my boss said, and took my hand. "Jesus," he mumbled, "we gotta get this staple off, but where the hell is the end of it?"

"It looks like it cut off the nail," his assistant said, peering over his shoulder. "Maybe we should leave it."

"No, wait, here, I think I've got it," I barely heard my boss say.

Whether there was a raffle book attached to me or not seemed unimportant. I felt dizzy and the room was spinning. I knew I had to sit down right away or I would definitely throw up. "I have to sit down," I said, and realized in that instant that the chair was too far away. I sat on the edge of a garbage can, and I was falling. My brain slipped into a fantasy world where Mike was giving me a kiss with his tongue, my mother was buying me a pink dress, and I was standing on my head at the circus.

Next thing I knew, my boss was slapping my face and my hand was in the running water of the sink, blood running into the drain. The booklet was no longer attached to it.

"Where are you, do you know?" asked my boss's assistant.

I looked at him like he was crazy. Now I could feel the pain in my finger, and it took all that was in me to keep from crying. "I'm at work. Print shop."

"What's your name?"

"Nancy. I'm fine, don't worry." I did my best to turn my hand over then so he wouldn't notice the scars which still showed on my wrist from the spring before.

Soon I was lying down on the floor by the door, waiting for the ambulance. The pain in my finger was unbelievable. I wanted to shut my eyes and try to think of other things, but then they'd worry that I was fainting again. I clenched my teeth and smiled. My boss held my uninjured hand and let me grip as hard as I wanted. I probably dug my nails into his palm, but he didn't complain.

When the ambulance came I tried to stand, thinking I should walk to it, but the men stopped me. They wanted to slide me onto a stretcher and bring me to the hospital that way. It seemed kind of dumb because I knew I could walk and I didn't feel faint at all, but they were in charge.

Ten minutes later, I lay on a bed in the emergency room, waiting for someone to get in touch with my parents. The hospital couldn't do anything until they had permission. Stupid, stupid, stupid. There I was, staring at the ceiling, in unbelievable pain, my finger sitting in a cup of something green which was supposed to make it feel better, and the skin floating on the surface like the whole top joint was about to come off, and my parents were nowhere to be found. Probably at the liquor store. God, it hurts, I thought. Definitely the most painful thing that ever happened to me.

Finally, my parents showed up. They were very gushy and sweet for the benefit of the hospital staff. I got X rays, and then it was decided that I should go to an orthopedist to have my top joint sewn back on. No bones were broken, except for a little piece at the tip which was crushed, and that couldn't be fixed.

My parents took me to a Dr. O'Hara, and he saw me right away. I felt like I was dying. Even so, I was worried about the night being ruined. Friday nights only came once a week, and I hated wasting them.

"Can Mike come over to see me tonight?" I asked my mother.

She sighed and rolled her eyes. "Just take it easy for one night, okay? You're hurt. No, he can't come over. You see him every week. You can miss this once." She turned and left the room in a whirl of blue cotton.

When the doctor came in, I gripped my father's hand. Dr. O'Hara had a needle of Novocain with him, and as he lifted my mangled and bloody finger I turned my head away. I was never able to stand the sight of needles. Poke, poke, prick, prick, prick, how many times was he going to stick me with that thing? As if he heard me thinking, he said, "Just one more time. Now careful, this is going to hurt, a lot."

The needle went into the soft flesh between my fingers, and I nearly screamed. Hurt a lot? It was going to kill me! Then the Novocain pumped into the finger, and I could feel it rise to the tip. When it got there, it felt like someone hit the end of my finger with a sledgehammer. I sucked in a

mouthful of air, hard. I was wrong about the pain earlier—
this was the most painful thing ever to happen to me.
Thank God it only lasted an instant.

The doctor stitched, and in fifteen minutes, he was finished. I had to take antibiotics, which sucked because I'd
heard the pill would then be ineffective. Shit, I thought,
this is the worst day. I had painkillers, too. I was told I
should keep my finger raised, so blood didn't flow to it
much, and it would hurt less. I should come back in four
days. Good-bye, have a nice day, talk to the nurse about the
bill, you have to give her the name of the print shop's
insurance company.

As I drove home with my parents, I wondered how long
they'd keep being nice to me and pestering me with their
questions and worried looks. I also wondered whether my
father had noticed the scars on my forearm while I was
getting the stitches. Lastly, I wondered whether I should
sneak out and see Mike that night, or if I should obey my
parents for once.

Chapter 17

Besides squashing my finger, school ended unevent-fully, except that my parents weren't too pleased about my grades. I wasn't thrilled with two C's and three B's either, especially since I'd wasted three weekends studying with Mike. But the first week of summer, only two days after getting my grades, Katie got tickets to see David Bowie at Giants Stadium, the August 1987 Glass Spider tour. The ticket was my birthday gift. The prospect of seeing Bowie lightened my mood, and I spent all of July and August until the concert counting the days.

John and Mike were going to the concert as well, which was good because Mike was driving us, but bad because they were so restrictive. Mike specifically said, "Nancy, there will be *no* weed in my car. *I* don't want to be arrested."

"How could you get arrested?" I argued, "What, do you think they're going to check every single car going into the lot?"

"No weed, or you can sell my ticket and take a train or something. I think John will agree with me, so don't count on him for anything."

"And what kind of person do you think I am, anyway? I *know* you're against me smoking, do you think I don't know that? You only tell me all the time! I would *never* smoke around you, I know it bothers you."

"I just wanted to make everything clear before we go. I know what you're like, but I want to make sure you'll inform Katie of the car rules."

"Katie would *never* smoke in someone's car who didn't smoke too. And she wouldn't smoke in front of John, either. Jeez, you guys have no respect for us, do you? We do have some judgment, you know. We're not assholes. I can't believe you would even mention that about weed. Like we wouldn't know it already. Like you haven't drilled it into my head a zillion times already."

"Just making sure, that's all. I didn't mean to offend you. Just making sure."

I was pissed that Mike trusted me so little after all the time we'd been going out. And I was sick of fighting all the time with Mike. It seemed like all we did was argue, make up, sleep together, and argue again. Even so, I told Katie what he'd said, though I knew she would never smoke in his car.

We intended to be good for once, but then Katie suddenly came up with one of her foolproof plans the night before the show. Of course we couldn't smoke, but we could eat. That's why she baked hash brownies the morning of the concert. One dozen, with fifty dollars worth of hash inside. Our only worry was whether we should tell Mike and John about the brownies. If we didn't, they might want to eat some. We thought of pretending they were burned or something, or even letting them eat and pretending they were perfectly normal brownies. How would we explain the grassy taste? Besides, if they found out, we might as well plan on walking home, so, in the parking lot of Giants Stadium, we told them. They laughed! But of course they did—it wasn't like we were smoking, it was a joke. We doubted we'd even be affected. Mike and

John preferred to drink their beer in the parking lot before we went in, and leave the brownies for Katie and me.

At three o'clock we were waiting on line at the stadium entrance, and memorizing the recorded announcement that repeated, "Welcome to Giants Stadium. It is stadium policy that . . ." and so on. Finally, the gate opened. We were on the floor, which was why we got there so early— we wanted to be real close to the stage. Unfortunately, the grass of the field was covered with black tarp, making the ninety-degree day feel even hotter. We could've passed out from the heat alone, sitting there for another four hours before the concert even started. Luckily, there were showers outside, lined up against one of the walls. Every five minutes we rushed to them and filled our cups with water. We had water fights and Katie and I ate brownies. By six o'clock, we were very high. I'd never been so high in my life—it felt so good! Mike and John were laughing too, but they didn't know that much of our gaiety was artificially induced. I hoped it would never wear off, it was so much fun. I thought we'd never stop laughing.

Lisa Lisa, the band which was opening for Squeeze, which was opening for Bowie, came onstage at seven o'clock, almost three hours after we'd eaten our first brownies. The crowd pushed forward and we had to move up or be trampled. I wasn't feeling so well anymore, and neither was Katie. I could tell by looking at her. I was scared. I wanted to cry because I could feel my control slowly slipping away and I couldn't stop it. I'd never felt so bad before.

Within fifteen minutes, I had to sit down, and Katie sat beside me. Mike and John were still standing. Oh God, I began to pray, I'm swaying now, and I can't stop. Oh God, what am I going to do. Katie can't help me. I can't help

Katie. Oh God, help me, oh God, help us. Billions of thick spaghetti strands pretending to be legs were marching on all sides of me. I saw sneakers—red high-tops and pink slippers and white heels. Oh, so many shoes and so much spaghetti—like a nightmare I used to have when I was little. I sat in a high chair and spaghetti was dumped over my head until I suffocated, a voice repeating, "Try it, you'll like it, try it, you'll like it."

Okay, stay cool. Breathe deeply. One, two, one, two, inhale, exhale, one, two. It wasn't like being drunk, when you know that the worst you'll do is vomit or pass out. I felt crazy—I didn't know if I'd cry, or pass out, or scream, or run naked through the spaghetti, or bang my head on the ground until my skull cracked open. But I'll be okay, I thought. I can make myself okay, this is only me, I can take care of this. I pulled on my short spiky hair, but couldn't really feel anything. But okay. Relax. Tried saying the alphabet backwards. I read somewhere about a girl doing that to keep control. Said Hail Marys. Tried to remember the words to a song I knew as a child—on top of spaghetti, all covered with cheese . . . Katie looked bad. I tried to stand, and almost vomited. Mike peered down from oh so far away and asked if I was okay. I couldn't speak, I just grabbed his sock the same time as Katie clawed John's pants leg. Next thing I knew, I was being carried out of the throngs of people. Mike, always my savior it seemed, propped me up beneath a shower and turned it on. Katie was next to me.

"Going for a walk," said the guys. "Don't move. Stay where you are until we get back. Don't move." Boy, did they look pissed. As water pattered on my head and dripped off my nose, I wondered without really caring whether they were going to leave us there for good. Take the car and disappear. I shut my eyes because everything was fuzzy and swimming and I couldn't see anyway.

In a short while, I couldn't tell how long, but before Mike and John came back, I started to feel better. The shower was a good idea. Everything came back into focus and I noticed that Squeeze was leaving the stage. Bowie would be on soon—at least we didn't miss that. I heard laughter. It was Katie. "Holy shit, look how far away we are! What a waste! We could've gotten here only a few minutes ago, and still gotten these seats!"

I laughed too. "I feel like I *did* get here only a few minutes ago!" I said. "Let's try to squirm back in." We'd forgotten about the guys for a second, but when we tried to stand, we both fell back again anyway.

Mike and John returned soon. Bowie lowered himself onstage and Katie and I clung to our boyfriends' arms so we could stand and move a little closer, though we stayed on the outskirts of the crowd. Moving too close made me queasy. Funny thing about the brownies. You don't ever think chocolate could hurt you, I mean, little kids eat it. But that's what was so dangerous, I guess. Smoking, you know your limit. But who knows his brownie limit?

As I grew more clearheaded, I started to notice the strange shit going on around me and I cringed. Near the wall, close to where Katie and I had been sitting, friends held each other's heads while they threw up. Lots of people leaned shoulder to shoulder or head to lap beneath the showers, and others were being carried out on stretchers. *Lots* of people on stretchers. God, I thought, we were so lucky! We were *so* close to being on one of those! Katie had decided to keep her hair short, so it was still fuzzy like a baby chick, and I rubbed my hand over it. She smiled at me. Thank God we fuck-ups had each other.

Sometime later, the concert ended, and I wasn't sure I comprehended everything but I thought it was good. It was Bowie, I must've had fun. Mike was real mad though. I wasn't sure if he'd leave me for good. I wouldn't have blamed him if he left me, I guess. But after all, he knew about the brownies. He had laughed, too.

When we got to the car, I reached into the belly of my army bag for a piece of glass, which I knew must be in there. Couldn't find it. Shit. Tears washed over my cheeks because nothing ever went right and I'd gone and ruined what should've been the best night of my life and I wasn't even going to have a boyfriend anymore. I turned in my seat to look at Katie for help, but she was asleep. Rubbing my fingernail up and down the side of my thigh, I soon joined her.

Chapter 18

"I guess you really blew it this time, Nancy," said Mike when he picked me up the next night.

I was relieved that he didn't sound angry, but I was annoyed that he seemed to pity me. "What're you talking about?" I asked.

"The concert. You were looking forward to it so much, and you didn't even get to see it. You probably don't even remember it."

"I saw it. I remember it!" What a lie. Oh yeah, I saw it—saw it on the big video screens they put up by the sides of the stage. And I could vaguely make out a figure in red who must've been Bowie. Remember it? Parts. Mostly, it felt like it was all a dream. I remembered he ended with "Modern Love." Or "Let's Dance." Or something from that album.

"I didn't *blow* it," I lied again. "I had a good time, at least for most of it. I didn't want to see those opening bands anyway."

Mike shrugged and we pulled into his driveway. We were watching a movie at his house because his parents had gone upstate for the weekend. As we walked up the front steps and inside, I suddenly felt nervous. Maybe it was because we'd already had one fight in our first five minutes together, and were sure to fight more if I wasn't careful. I was glad I'd brought something to calm me down. "Excuse me," I said, "I have to go to the bathroom."

I toted my army bag into the yellow-walled room with me and set it on the closed toilet seat. It had a peach-colored shag cover on it, matching the towels. Clustered on the back of the toilet were peach and yellow scallop-shaped soaps. My bathroom at home had a dark gray ring around the tub and the bowl of the toilet, which had only a seat on it because my father never got around to reattaching the plastic cover. The only soap we had was Ivory, stuck in a gooey puddle to the edge of the sink. Once again I wondered, what does this guy see in me? I took a cologne bottle from my bag and swallowed the three inches of vodka in it. Putting my mouth under the faucet, I washed down the drink with water and left the bathroom. Much better.

We were watching *The Shining* and less than halfway through, it started to get fuzzy. Boy, that vodka really hit me! Must've been because I didn't have any dinner, but I had to watch my weight or Mike wouldn't go out with me anymore. Especially after my screw-up at the concert. "I'm so sorry," I said, pushing my face against his neck.

"About what?" he asked, and I laughed.

"The concert. I'm a mess, I know. I'm not good for you, I know. Why do you put up with me? What do you see in me?" I reached for his crotch.

Mike pushed me back against the couch and bit my neck. Great, I thought, I need some more marks on my skin like I need another drink. Jesus. "You have a beautiful ass," Mike said, squeezing it. Good thing I didn't have dinner.

Untying his sweatpants I said, "Not as great as yours," and pulled the pants to his knees.

In less than five minutes he was done, and didn't bother pretending he wasn't. I was a little too tipsy to care, but I sensed something was about to happen, and I was glad I'd had that drink. "Nancy, you know I love you," he said.

"What's that supposed to mean?"

He looked at the ceiling. "What do you mean, 'What's that supposed to mean?' It means I love you, okay?"

"Okay. Sorry. I love you too."

"But I've been thinking about us, and . . ."

Oh, here it is. The moment we've all been waiting for, folks. The moment of truth. The moment of ditching. Post-orgasm, of course.

Mike was silent, and for a minute, at least, we just looked at each other. Then I said, "You want to see someone else. Are you already seeing her? What's going on? How long have you been seeing her?"

"There's someone I'm interested in, but that's not the reason—"

"Who? Who is it?"

"It doesn't matter, that's not the point. It has nothing to do with—"

"Who is it? Is it Amy? Someone from school? Someone—"

"It doesn't *matter*, I just—"

"Why won't you tell me who? Is she prettier than me? Is it because of the concert? I said I was sorry! It was your fault, too, you know, you said—"

"Would you be *quiet* please, and let me talk? Look, it's nothing serious, or I would have told you sooner. I don't even know if we're going to start seeing each other. I don't even know if she's interested. I just wanted you to know about it. I still want to see you. I still love *you*, I just think we're a little too serious. You obviously want your freedom to hang out with Katie and do the weird shit you do. I know you think I tie you down. I don't want to do that anymore, okay?"

Oh wow. I always knew, and maybe it was what I always wanted, but I never really expected it to happen. I wanted to be hard and tough like Katie would be, but I was crying anyway. Without even thinking, I thrust my forearm into my mouth and bit, hard. Mike yanked my teeth back, but not quick enough. My jaws didn't break the skin but there was a purple oval of teeth marks, and I'd bitten hard enough to push blood up through the center of the bite, right through the pores, I guess. It was kind of cool looking.

Mike wrapped his arms around me and I could smell his aftershave. "Mike, I'm sorry, I couldn't help it. You took me by surprise. The thought of you with someone else . . ."

He kissed my forehead and then tickled me under my armpits. When I laughed, he smiled. "There's the girl I fell in love with!" he said. "There's that beautiful smile! You don't smile enough anymore, Nancy. We used to have fun."

"How can you expect me to smile when you just told me you want to fuck someone else?" I blurted out and bit my lip.

"I didn't say I was sleeping with anyone," Mike said, rubbing his foot against my leg. "Can we just forget I ever said anything? There isn't anyone else but you, really there isn't. I was just thinking out loud, and I wasn't thinking too clearly."

Kissing Mike gently on the lips and smiling, I said, "Excuse me," and went into the bathroom to wipe my eyes and rinse the bite on my arm. I felt a little guilty for manipulating Mike the way I did. Although I really had been upset, I couldn't help but think I'd bitten my arm because I knew how Mike loved to feel needed. It was like Katie shaving her head—too pitiful for any guy to leave.

I returned to the bathroom, trying to look pitiful, but smiling because Mike still loved me. Fuzz appeared on the television screen as the videotape ended, and Mike gently reached under my shirt. I stopped smiling so I could kiss him.

Guilt turned out to be a very effective means of keeping Mike and me together. For a week it was like the first week we were going out. I even stopped smoking cigarettes and dressing punk when I went anywhere with him. Unfortunately, one week was all it lasted. We began to drift apart again. Even though every night he said he loved me, the summer was nearly over, and I wasn't sure we could make it through another school year.

Katie's mother went away for Labor Day weekend, and Saturday night, Katie decided to have a party. I thought it could be like old times for Mike and me, when we used to go to his friends' pool parties and barbecues, but Mike wanted to go barhopping with his friends from school. I fought with him a little about it, but I let him go. Katie's and my friends weren't his friends anyway, and without him at the party, I was free to do what I wanted, drug-wise. I swore to myself that if he came, I would be mellow, not drinking or smoking or anything. That was another thing I'd found about sex—it was better straight. But Mike wasn't there, so why not get blasted?

I was on my fourth beer and someone was passing a bowl. Suddenly, I didn't want it, which was unusual for me. I passed it on, despite teasing. But what did I care what these people thought, anyway? I didn't even know them, except for Andy, and I didn't know him very well. Katie and John were there, but they left. Gone over twenty minutes, I noticed, looking at my watch.

The party was mostly guys, or girls with their boyfriends —I seemed to be the only single girl present. The guys were starting to annoy me. I'd heard about eight pick-up lines, and they were still coming when I popped open my sixth beer. There was a guy sitting on the couch across from me who pulled his shirt up over his nipple and gestured toward the door. Oh, gimme a *break*!

I wished Mike were there. Suddenly I felt jealous of the few couples climbing all over each other, and I wanted to be doing that with Mike. He might want to see other girls, but I was perfectly satisfied with the way things were. Maybe he'll decide he misses me tonight and stop by to surprise me, I hoped. I was spending the night at Katie's, so for once I wouldn't have to be rushed home when we were through. We could wake up together, wouldn't that be nice?

I was sitting in a worn armchair in Katie's living room. Lighting a cigarette, the match flew out of my hand and into Andy's lap.

"Watch where you throw those things!" he warned, and I laughed. I was very drunk. Glad I didn't smoke any weed. Glad I was still sober enough to stay away from the sleazos who were still trying to pick me up. I figured I'd stick by Andy—he seemed to be the only safe person around, what with a wife and baby at home. It was hard for me to believe Cheri's ploy had actually worked. I wondered whether she actually let Andy go to the party, or whether he sneaked out of his house like I usually did from mine.

One of Katie's kittens, Sambo, pounced on my lap. Absently I petted it and talked to Andy, who sat on the floor next to my chair. Since we didn't know each other well, the conversation soon got boring, but I was trying to avoid everyone else at the party, so what could I do? Pet the kitten more intensely.

It grew close to three in the morning and Katie still hadn't come home. Nearly everyone had passed out, except for two guys sitting in the doorway of the kitchen, one strumming a guitar, the other singing off-key. I must have blacked out for a minute or something, because I didn't know where Andy was. He must've gone home, thank God. He was getting on my nerves. But at least he kept me from being picked up.

I was exhausted, so I stood up and placed the sleeping kitten on the chair seat. Carefully, I went upstairs to Katie's bedroom. I was very tired, and I guess I was still somewhat under the effects of the alcohol because as soon as I lay down, I fell asleep. Passed out is maybe a better term. I was still wearing my miniskirt and purple tank top.

I was dreaming about Mike, dreaming that he came to the party right after I went upstairs and started taking my clothes off. He was kissing my neck, and he pushed my tank up. I leaned my head back and moaned as he pulled it up, up, over my matted hair. Very slowly, he unsnapped my bra, and put both hands on my chest. I was smiling happily as he unzipped my skirt and started pulling it down. He kissed my neck again, this time biting it, hard.

"Ouch," I said, and suddenly I was awake and a little confused because it wasn't a dream and I wasn't alone, but Andy had his hand on my crotch, and we were both almost naked. It took me a second to figure out what was going on, and in that time things began moving very fast.

I tried to push Andy away, which I thought would be easy since he was so skinny, but then I was no bodybuilder either.

Andy looked pissed at my sudden resistance, and when he grabbed my wrists so I'd stop hitting him, he dug his nails into my skin. "Come on, Nancy. You've wanted me since the day we met, just like Katie."

"Katie never wanted you! I never wanted you! You're married!" I said and then started to gag, like I was going to throw up. Fighting while you're wasted is hardly ever a good idea, and I had a weak stomach.

Andy put both my hands over my mouth and leaned his naked body closer to mine. I couldn't wiggle free, so I squeezed my eyes shut and tried to imagine myself anywhere but under Andy's bony body.

Suddenly, someone was banging on the door. "Go away," Andy yelled.

The door opened and it was John and Katie. Katie asked if everything was okay, and I couldn't even speak, but I was able to shake my head. Andy was already zipping his pants, and as he picked up his shirt, John was already pulling him out the door. When Katie came to my side, I didn't know what to say. I couldn't even move to put my clothes back on, I was so humiliated. What if I hadn't woken up? How long had he been there touching me before I woke up? I could see him telling all his friends tomorrow what a great lay I was and how much I wanted him. Katie said it wasn't my fault and dressed me. I rolled over and faced the wall, dazed and maybe a little drunk. Soon I fell back to sleep with Katie sleeping on the floor next to me. John slept downstairs on the couch to make sure Andy didn't come back.

The next day I woke up and wasn't hung over, but I wanted to be. I wanted to hurt physically, so I wouldn't have to think. It wasn't my fault, was it? Katie said no, but I didn't know if she meant it. I shouldn't have worn that skirt or that shirt. I didn't think I led Andy on, but maybe I did. No. I didn't touch him, or insinuate anything. All I did was pet the kitten. My legs were crossed all night, and I thought Andy had gone home. Damn it, why did I drink? I kept thinking. Oh God, it was the perfume. If I wasn't going to be with Mike, why did I bother? Shit, I thought, I'm such a fuck-up. Shit, shit, shit! My God, how was I going to tell Mike?

Chapter 19

It wasn't my fault, I was sure it wasn't my fault. Labor Day, two days after Katie's party I was still telling myself that. I'd been over it and over it in my mind, and I was finally convinced that it couldn't have been my fault. I didn't *ask* to be raped! Even if I *had* led him on, which I didn't, he had no right.

". . . and I was *sleeping*," I told Mike, pushing tears up into my eyebrows, trying to make it look like I was only wiping away sweat. It was ninety-six degrees out, and we were sitting on the deck in his backyard. He sat leaning back on a lawn chair and I was leaning back on him, sitting between his legs.

"Ouch," he said, moving me forward a little. "You're crushing me. It's too hot for this. Why don't you sit there." He gestured to the chair next to him. His cat peered up at me from the green vinyl seat, obviously thinking the same thing I was—"Are you out of your fucking mind? What is *wrong* with you?"

I got up and moved. Tiger would probably be more comforting to me anyway. I scratched him under his chin and he purred. Kind of like Katie's Sambo, which reminded me —didn't a certain boyfriend of mine owe me a little sympathy? "You've passed out before, you know what it's like," I said, still fighting tears.

"But I managed to keep my clothes on."

I smacked my hand against the back of the chair. "I didn't *want* it to happen! Can't you see that?"

"According to John, he wasn't even sure you wanted the guy to leave. He thought maybe he and Katie were interrupting you."

"Jesus *Christ*, I was *raped*! What kind of person are you? I was *raped*! That's r-a-p-e-d, *raped*!"

"You said he never forced intercourse," Mike said, looking away.

I stared at him, my mouth hanging open for several seconds. Then I said, "You're fucking unbelievable! I called the Rape Hotline, you know. They said it's rape if the victim considers it rape. *I'm* the victim and I call it rape!"

Mike didn't seem to know what to say. I almost felt bad for him because he looked so confused, but I wanted his sympathy first.

"It still hasn't been working between us, you know. I tried, but it isn't any good anymore," Mike said after a long period of silence.

"Fuck you!"

"Look, if you didn't have anything to do with it, why do you sound so guilty?"

"My *God*, I thought I *knew* you! I was *wrong*! Who *are* you? *Look* at this." I poked my finger into the large purple hickey on my neck. It looked like a miniature map of Long Island. "I don't even like when *you* do this to me, do you think I would let someone else, if I was awake and aware of what was happening?"

"I *know* you weren't 'awake' or 'aware,' but that's a lot of the problem, isn't it? I can't baby-sit you forever, Nancy. I just can't take it anymore, I'm sorry. And don't try any of your damn tricks either. I'm sick of that, too. You can't keep me with guilt or pity. It isn't working for me anymore."

"What's the matter, aren't I a good enough lay? Boy, I was for Andy, let me tell you!" I couldn't stop myself from crying now. I was out of control. Crazed, I pulled my shirt over my head. "Come on, give me your best shot! Oh, but better make me real drunk first. Better let me pass out. I'm better when I'm asleep, you know that. You probably called Andy today, he probably told you how good I am when I'm asleep. No participation, but who needs that? Certainly not the almighty *men* of this world, that's for sure!"

"Put your shirt on," Mike said. "Don't be an idiot. Look, it's not just this, it's lots of things. We don't get along like we used to. You'd rather pass out with Katie, and I have my friends at school." Mike gripped his hands so tightly on the vinyl seat cushion, his tan skin looked white.

Just like my scars, I thought, squirming back into my shirt. "So, do they do shit like you do? Will your new slut let you pinch her wrists between one of your hands while you pound her? You think you can do better than *me*?"

"I'll take you home now. Maybe sometime when you're more calm, we can talk this over like human beings."

"I *am* calm!" Sobbing uncontrollably, I stood and threw my arms around Mike's middle, burying my face in his chest. "Please, please don't do this to me! I'll be better, I promise! I won't do any drugs, I won't even drink. I'll quit smoking cigarettes."

"Nancy."

"Don't do this to me. I'll kill myself if you leave me, I really will this time. I love you too much. Why does everyone always want to hurt me? You're all I have, besides Katie, and she's got John."

"Not for long, believe me." Mike peeled me off of him. "Listen, Nancy, we're no good for each other anymore. You know that too, if you'll just admit it to yourself. I think you need help."

"So *help* me, you bastard!"

"I *can't.* I love you, but I can't. Maybe you should talk to your parents. They're not really so bad; they only do what they think's best. I know they really love you. You need real help, from someone more qualified than me."

"I don't need a shrink, I need *you!*"

"If money's a problem, talk to me. I'm sure I can help. But I can't go out with you anymore, and I can't feel guilty about it either. You're not my fault. Come on, I'm taking you home."

"One last kiss?"

"I'm taking you home."

Chapter 20

When I got home I walked very calmly and slowly past my mother and the TV. I was careful not to let any emotion show, not to let anyone see there was something wrong. Eventually my parents would probably find out about Mike and then I'd be embarrassed, because they were sure to say, "We told you so," but I couldn't deal with that tonight. I had to keep control. Why did it seem like I was always fighting to do that, to keep control? For normal people, it came naturally, didn't it? I reached my room and flopped onto my bed, crying. I hate him, I hate him, I hate him! I cried mutely into my pillow, what an asshole, he had *no right*! I did everything for him, I gave him everything I could, and he never loved me. God, I'm such a fool, believing it when he said he loved me all those times, when it was really all one big lie! *Fuck him!*

I took the glass out of my night table drawer. Cut down my arm—I'm bad—cut up the arm—evil, bad, screw-up—cut down—I fuck up everyone's lives—cut up—shithead—why doesn't someone just shoot me?—cut down—what the fuck am I doing? Again, I knew I was only messing around. It was dumb—it dawned on me that no one was going to give me any sympathy for some scratches—my parents wouldn't even notice, and Mike wouldn't even see me, much less my scratches. I was bad for him, it was time he got the chance to lead a normal life with a good girl.

I threw the glass at my wall and started punching my pillow. Then I moved my chair in front of my door, the top rung jammed under the door handle so it couldn't open. I returned to the pillow. I punched it, I hit it on the wall, I pounded on my mattress.

"Quiet up there!" shouted my mother from downstairs.

I went even more wild, ripping the pillow open and tearing out stuffing which I shoved into my mouth to keep from screaming. I punched my forehead as hard as I could, and then pounded it against the wall. The pain felt good—it felt like finally I was getting what I deserved. The violence felt good because I was so violent inside, and suddenly it was being forced outside too. No more lies, let it all hang out.

I was bad, and all the cutting in the world wasn't punishment because it never hurt much, it looked worse than it really was. But now I'd really hurt, and that would be good. Finally, I was getting back for all I did. For all I'd gotten away with. No one else would do it to me, for me, so I had to punish myself.

I wondered, would I have the nerve to jump out the window? The pounding of blood in my head *hurt*, it hurt so much. I wanted it to stop, but the pain was never going to stop. It was too late, I screwed up everything, and now the pain would *be* me, forever.

There was pounding on the door, it had to be my mother, or my father, or fuck, I didn't know. I lit a cigarette, even though I wasn't allowed to smoke and I didn't even know if my parents realized that I still did. But no more lies, I didn't want to lie anymore. All out in the open.

I pushed the cigarette into my arm. Lit another, pushed into my arm. Hey, a thought flashed through my burning head, this is interesting. How long before my parents would find a way in? They were calling to me, but it sounded far away. I didn't answer. I figured unless they'd gotten some real good drugs, I was never coming out. Except maybe by window, but I didn't think that would work. I wasn't that high up, I'd probably only break a leg or something. I was sick of fake suicides, and stupid grasps for pity. Mike was right about that—I was an idiot. But no more, I thought—from now on, it's all for real.

I lit another cigarette, leaving it in my mouth this time, and swung my arm back, hard against my headboard. There was a big rusty nail sticking out about an inch, and beautiful, it went right into my arm, just above my wrist. I pulled myself free from the nail and swung the other arm. Direct hit. Blood spurting out like I pressed the "on" button of a water fountain. I started hitting more, harder, faster. Blood was everywhere, and suddenly my arms were grabbed from behind, pulled back. I looked up and screamed, "Get off!"

He dragged me out of my room anyway, and then I didn't remember anymore until maybe an hour, maybe a day, maybe a week later, when I woke up in some hospital.

Chapter 21

I lay in my white bed, in my white room, and looked at my white ceiling. I wanted a cigarette. Get me the fuck out of here, God, I thought. I didn't belong there—if I wanted to die, they couldn't stop me. But I didn't want to die anymore anyway. I thought about Katie being all alone, and I realized *she* needed me. I wasn't bad to her. I was good for her like she was good for me. If Mike was telling the truth then John would be sliming her soon and she'd need me even more. It'd be just us two, and I had to stick around for that. Everything would be okay when it was down to just us two.

I turned my head. There were two bouquets of flowers sitting on my night table. One was daisies, from Katie. I kissed the petals of one flower. The other bunch was from Mike. Angry, I ripped them from the vase. The packet of powder which was supposed to be put into the water to make them live longer fell onto my bed. I threw the flowers against the wall. Smiling, I picked up the packet of white powder. I remembered when Katie and I used to sniff Tylenol, for kicks.

Wonder what would happen if I sniffed flower-powder? I looked around. No, of course no one was watching. Laughing quietly, I pulled open the plastic and dumped the powder onto my sheet. I rolled up the card from Katie's flowers and put one end in my nose. Sniff.

* * *

The next day, when school would be starting for Katie and the rest of my peers, I sat in my psychiatrist's office, playing chess. He'd let me win the first game, and we'd played in silence. Now, as he slowly advanced toward my king, he was pestering me with questions.

"What about how rotten you treat yourself?" asked Dr. Pear-Buttock (a name affectionately given to him by my fellow loonies).

I shrugged, taking his bishop with my queen.

"What about how rotten you treat Katie?"

Now I looked up. "Excuse me?"

"Katie. For a best friend, you treat her pretty rotten. Check."

I sat quietly for a minute, staring at the chessboard. Moving my king to safety, I tried to pretend I didn't hear him. Then I mentally counted to ten, telling myself, it's okay, don't get angry. Just cool it. Mellow. Relax.

It didn't work.

"I would *never, never* have hurt Katie!" I cried, slamming my fist on the table and toppling several chess pieces.

"You let her use dangerous narcotics. You let her cut herself."

"She's old enough to do what she wants."

"You *like* to see her hurt, don't you . . ."

"That's stupid."

"Misery loves company. You want her to hurt because you do."

"Cut it out. You don't know anything. Talk to her *mother, she* makes Katie hurt. Like my parents do. *They're* what's so *miserable!*"

Dr. Pear-Butt tried to keep badgering me, but I shut up. I couldn't talk—I was too busy slowing down the cogs in my brain so my head would stop hurting and I'd stop hearing his voice over and over. I didn't believe him. I knew I couldn't stop and we needed the cutting to survive. Still, a part of me argued that we *did* freak out at the Bowie concert and I *did* get raped when . . . well, it didn't matter, I told myself. Katie and I always knew what we were doing.

For the entire month of September I spent two hours a day with Pear-Butt. I got to be pretty good at chess, but other than that we didn't make much progress. But then it dawned on me that if I didn't start showing visible improvement, I'd never get out.

I enjoyed being in the hospital at first—all I *had* to do was visit my shrink. The rest of the time me and the other young crazies smoked cigarettes, played video games in the arcade they had on the second floor, and hung out in front of the TV. The other kids were cool, too. Most weren't really crazy—I think I was the craziest there, and I wasn't crazy at all. Mostly everyone was in there for crimes. The courts put them in the hospital at least temporarily if their parents could afford it. They had to commit an awful lot of crimes before they had to go to any reform place. Kids, the general assumption was, were only bad because they were screwed up in the head. If they weren't screwed up, they'd be perfectly content to mind their manners and wear pink bows in their hair until they were twenty-one. It was funny, too, considering the shit they did.

It was amazing what kids our age could get away with. One of the guys was in for going around pretending to collect for Muscular Dystrophy. He wanted money to buy a case of beer. And he actually got eight dollars before someone turned him in! He strutted around his clean, neat suburban neighborhood with his long, greasy hair and torn T-shirt, and people gave him money. Unbelievable.

Despite the easy life and the neat people I met, I began to get lonely. I missed Katie and even Mike, neither of whom were permitted to visit me. Phone calls were also limited to family members. Missing so much school bugged me too, surprisingly enough. Most of the people I met seemed to care only about passing their GED's so they could work as mechanics or secretaries. As little direction as I had in my life, I knew I wanted to eventually work at a job that had a little more promise than that. Even as I'd let my grades drop while I was in school, I'd still always assumed I'd go to college. So, I wondered, staring blankly at the TV one afternoon in late September, what am I doing spending the first month of my junior year in a mental hospital?

For the next two weeks, I concentrated on telling Dr. Pear-Butt everything he wanted to hear. The more I wanted to get out, the more I noticed that the food in the hospital sucked. The people were getting on my nerves, the chairs were uncomfortable and the hallways smelled like ammonia. I even began to look forward to my parents' visits.

My parents helped me convince the hospital staff to send me home for Halloween weekend. They even dressed up to come get me, and neither smelled of booze. I sniffed real hard too, figuring they just wanted to make a good impression on my Pear-Butt shrink, and would crack open a bottle when we got home.

I didn't talk in the car, but only stared out the window at the leaves in their fall colors. When we got to my house, I wondered if they'd make me rake up the bright fallout from our two maple trees.

"Sit down, Nancy," my father said before the screen door had even swung shut behind me.

I tried to look carefree as I plopped onto the couch. My

parents sat across the coffee table from me. Their faces seemed painted on, like Barbie and Ken.

My father cleared his throat. "Nancy—"

"No, wait. I have something to say first," my mother interrupted. "Nancy, your father and I have joined Alcoholics Anonymous."

I couldn't help it. I giggled. I don't think it was what she said—maybe it was how she said it or how she looked or how all *three* of us looked. Anyway, I shut up real quick, but not quick enough. My father leaned forward angrily, and opened his mouth to speak.

My mother hushed him. "Please, Nancy. We're trying. I know you're angry and hurt, and you probably don't even like us, but we're trying. God, if you only knew how we're trying."

I could feel a lump in my throat, and it made me angry. How dare they try to manipulate me! How dare they try to make *me* feel sorry for *them*! I looked down at my hands and concentrated on my fingernails to make sure I wouldn't cry. They couldn't make me do that.

My mother, however, had no qualms about letting the water flow over her cheeks. "You know what I see in you?" she said, her voice breaking a little. "I see me. *Me.* If you think you're special, I can tell you, you're not. I was *just like you!* I *was!* No, don't smile. I'm very serious now. I know what it's like to want to, to need to stand out—I had seven brothers and sisters, remember? I know all about rebellion and drinking and smoking because *I was you.* I know what it's like to have alcoholic parents, and I never wanted it for you. I just don't know what happened, but something screwed up in my great, cocky plan and here I am, an alcoholic bitch with a daughter as foolish as I was."

My mother began sobbing loudly again, and my father

moved to comfort her. Tears were now pushing over my lower lashes, and I quickly wiped them, pretending I was coughing. "I'm sorry. I'm going to bed, I'm tired," I said, looking at my shoes and heading for the stairs. I knew the appropriate thing to do would've been to go around the coffee table and tearfully hug my parents, but I couldn't. Hearing them cry made me pity them, and pitying them made me sick. I started up the stairs.

"I know what it's like to want to die, too!" my mother called. "I don't want you to be like me! I don't want you to die!"

Maybe she kept yelling stuff, I didn't know because I was quickly secreted in my room with my door shut, radio on, cigarette lit, and eyes squeezed tight to hold in the tears.

Chapter zz

Saturday morning I got up at nine, then got on my bike and rode to Katie's house without saying good-bye to my parents. They were still sleeping, and I knew they wouldn't want me at Katie's house—or out at all. Katie was really happy to see me.

We ate breakfast in the kitchen because her mother wasn't home. Then went upstairs to her room. She started telling me all about things I'd missed, which wasn't much, except that she decided to let her hair grow. It was almost down to her ears. But even with nothing special to talk about, we lay on her floor, talking for hours. Suddenly, Katie sat up. She crawled to her bureau and opened the bottom drawer, pulling out a small plastic bag.

"Weed?" I asked.

She shook her head. "Better. Mushrooms. Let's eat!"

"Oh, Katie, I don't know. I've been thinking, maybe we should quit this stuff. It's not that I don't want to, but I'm starting to think it's bad for us. And have we ever spent time together being straight? Maybe we should try it, and if we don't like it, then we can do the other stuff again."

"Shit, what's that place doing to you? We *got* to get you out of there for good! It's screwing up your head! This stuff is *good* for you! Or at least it's fun. Don't get me wrong, I think it'd be cool to hang out straight sometime, but why not wait until we have to—when there's no drugs to be had? While they're here, might as well use 'em. Children are straight in China, you know!"

She was right, as usual. I was amazed she didn't get better grades in school, considering how smart she was. It wasn't like we *couldn't* have a good time straight, too, it was just that, why bother? We could save that for a special occasion. Oh, but mushrooms?

"Katie, they're so gross tasting, isn't there anything else?"

"No. Come on, quit bitching. Here, I'll feed you."

Katie opened a bag of Cheez Doodles and shoved one in my mouth. Before I could chew, she threw in a mushroom cap. I chewed them together while she swallowed one of her own. She stuffed two more caps in my mouth. Cheez Doodle, mushroom, Cheez Doodle, mushroom. It didn't kill the horrible taste, and once I gagged, but we managed to finish the eighth between us.

We lay on her floor. In a half hour, we were chewing Velamints to curb our nausea—my stomach felt like it had a hand on it, twisting it like you twist the top of a garbage bag before tying it shut. I imagined that's what my insides were like, a garbage bag.

We stared at the stucco ceiling, watching the plaster ripple like tiny white waves. Bubbling and popping and rippling, the ceiling moved back and forth and down the sides of the wall. Cool. Katie shoved another Velamint into my mouth and I almost threw up, but the feeling passed. I reached for her hand, and we held on tight to each other. You and me against the world, I thought. You and me and the moving ceiling and the sinking floor and the yellow dots floating outside the window. Don't need anyone else. And tomorrow we'll do this again, but straight. We could do anything together.

Maybe I wouldn't go back to that dumb hospital like I

was supposed to at the end of the weekend. I didn't need it anyway. I didn't belong there—I didn't commit any crimes. I wanted to be with Katie, because she did more good for me than any idiot shrink who couldn't make any ceilings move. No, I'd just lie there on the floor with my best friend until I died, and that'd be good, and that's all I needed. I was sick of people calling us crazy when it was they who were fucked up.

I let my head flop to the side, away from the moving, dipping ceiling, and stared at Katie. She was beautiful. God, I was so lucky to have her as my best friend. As I watched her nostrils flare in and out while she breathed, Katie suddenly let her head flop toward me. We lay with our noses touching for a long time. At least it felt like a long time. I couldn't tell.

My love for Katie was overwhelming, and I felt like I was going to burst. The floor was rippling beneath me. As I flung an arm over Katie for support, I gently, without thinking why or where or how or what, put my lips against hers. It wasn't sexual—we were too wasted to feel anything physically—but she swallowed me up, and all I could think was how great it was to be like one person with her.

Katie and I remained next to each other on the floor for I don't know how long, but it couldn't have been more than an hour or two because we were still wasted when the doorbell rang below us. It made us giggle. Hoping the visitor would leave, we stayed on the floor. I, for one, felt too gooey to move. But the doorbell persisted, soon accompanied by impatient knocking. Although the sound seemed very far away, I motioned slowly to Katie that I'd get it.

Smiling for no particular reason, I half-stumbled down the stairs. Grabbing the railing for support would have been impractical because it didn't look too sturdy. Besides, its rippling and wriggling made it impossible to even catch. It was all I could do just to find the steps with my feet. Gradually, I reached the door, and somehow managed to open it.

Mike, stepping inside, put his hand under my sweaty armpit to steady my swaying. Just like him to spoil all the fun, I thought.

"What do *you* want?" I said, flopping onto the wildly patterned sofa. I tried to pick one of the cherry-and-yellow flowers to put in my hair, but it wouldn't come off the fabric.

"Your parents called. They thought you might be with me, but I knew you had to be over here."

"So?"

"They're worried."

"So?" I stared at Mike intently. "You know, I never noticed how your eyes change colors like that."

Mike took my hand and held it for a while before speaking. "They're sorry, you know."

"I've heard."

"I'm sorry too." Mike shifted his gaze to the floor and wiped at his eyes. What *is* it with everyone? I thought. *I* was the one supposed to cry all the time.

I giggled, and Mike looked up.

"I'm really sorry, Nancy," he said, his face contorted and looking like a giant raisin. I couldn't tell if it was just me, or if he really was scrunching his features, so I reached forward and touched his forehead. Felt like a raisin.

"Little feverish. Take two aspirin and call me in the morning." I got up to go back upstairs, but Mike only gripped my hand tighter.

I stared at him.

He continued, "I know it wasn't your fault. I'm sorry. I think I still love you."

Now his face got really contorted, and I knew it wasn't just the mushrooms telling me this because I could see the tears. At first I thought I should run upstairs and lock Katie's door behind me, light a cigarette, and turn on the radio. But this was Mike, not my parents. He might have been a straitlaced stiff who couldn't understand me, but I was pretty sure I still loved him, though I was mad as hell at him.

I fell on him, freeing my hand and beating his chest and arms with my fists until I was crying so hard I couldn't see. Suddenly I felt sick and ran to the bathroom to vomit. Mike followed me, and when I was done, wiped my mouth with toilet paper. Sitting on the blue-tiled floor, he cradled me in his arms and apologized again and again, until I believed him. I knew I might be fooling myself, but I believed him.

I was too wasted to have any concept of time, but it must have been several minutes before Mike whispered that he'd better take me home because my parents were worried. I was so exhausted, I didn't care. Whatever he wanted to do was fine, as long as I could sleep. My eyes were already drooping nearly shut as I shuffled to the front door, Mike's arm steadying me. Suddenly I remembered Katie, splayed across her rug upstairs.

"I'll be back," I said hoarsely to Mike, pushing off of him to gain some of the momentum I figured I'd need to get up the stairs. Banging my shins often on the steps, I finally made it to Katie's room.

"I thought you were gone for good," Katie said, her face wet with tears and her nose running. No longer stretched out on the floor, she now sat in the window, one leg dangling outside. "I'm looking at the sky," she continued, suddenly giggling, "and all the pretty rainbows of color. I'm waiting for a leprechaun, you know, those green men. I'm waiting for him to come get the pot of gold." Katie began laughing harder, and I laughed with her. Rushing to her, I gave her a quick hug and kiss and said, "I have to go home. My parents, you know."

Katie nodded, kissed my forehead, and giggled some more. I felt bad leaving her, since we hadn't seen each other for so long, but I knew Mike was waiting, and I was kind of hoping that if I did what he said, everything would be okay. He'd love me for always and I'd love him. Or at least he'd make me feel better.

"Tomorrow!" I yelled up from the bottom of the stairs. Then, as Mike and I crunched up the gravel driveway to his car, I yelled to Katie's head, protruding from the window like a turtle's from its shell. "I'll call you tomorrow!" But she didn't hear me or wasn't listening. She kept staring at the sky, and I got into Mike's car and promptly passed out.

Chapter 23

Instead of taking me straight home, Mike let me sleep off the aftermath of the mushrooms in the front seat of his car. At about five, he finally dropped me at my house, still fuzzy-headed, but straight as an arrow. My parents were so sweet and understanding—they hugged me when I came in and said things like, "Did you have fun? How's Katie? How's her mother? We were worried, maybe next time you could leave a note, just to let us know where you are, just so we don't worry. What would you like for dinner?

It all made me want to puke. I couldn't figure out what they were trying to pull, and I wondered how long it would last. Still, I was happy not to be fighting. Even if the sweetness were insincere, I'd take it any day over drunken swears.

We ate a friendly, though silent, pizza dinner and, still worn out from the day's prelunch partying, I went to bed right after dinner.

My mother came up to say good night and to tell me she loved me. I almost rolled my eyes, but yawned instead. She tiptoed out, and when I knew she was back downstairs, I sat up in bed and lit a cigarette. Smoking slowly, I thought about the weekend so far. Mike said he loved me, so did my mother. How long would it last? I wasn't stupid enough to believe that presto-chango, they'd all been magically transformed overnight to the best Mommy, Daddy and boyfriend in the world. But it was obvious they were trying. I wondered what it would take from me to keep them that way. I also wondered what little screw-up of mine would magically transform everyone back into what they were before.

Then there was Katie. God! I missed her. I shouldn't have left her—I should've spent the whole weekend at her house. The thing about Katie was I knew she needed me. I couldn't really say that about anyone else, in fact I still thought mostly everyone's lives would be much easier without me. I wondered what would happen between Katie and me if Mike and I got back together, or if my parents and I got together for the first time.

Oh, who gives a shit? I thought, crushing my cigarette inside my night table drawer and scrunching under my sheet. Katie and I would outlast everyone, no matter what. If I wanted to quit drugs, maybe even cutting, maybe even cigarettes, she'd do it with me. We were like one person, so if my life got better, hers would too.

Putting my thumb in my mouth, I shut my eyes. Suddenly I remembered how mad my mother had been when I was in seventh grade and she found out I still sucked my thumb. Reluctantly, I removed my thumb. Before I could think how uncomfortable I was without it in my mouth, I fell asleep.

Chapter 24

Sunday morning I didn't wake up until noon. I was surprised my parents didn't drag me from my bed to the church for early morning Mass, and wondered what was up. Remembering I had to be back at the hospital by four, I quickly got dressed and went downstairs to call Katie. My parents were sitting quietly at the dining room table, staring into their coffee cups. When I passed through to the kitchen, they looked up at me, staring as intently as they had at their coffee.

Uh-oh, I thought, here comes the lecture I missed yesterday. Hoping to slip out of the house before it came, I quickly dialed Katie's number. Ten rings, no answer.

"Get your stuff together, Nan, we have to go back to the hospital," my father said.

My eyes widened with bafflement and anger. So this was the catch. No lecture, but no Katie either. "But I made plans," I said.

"With Katie?" my mother whispered.

I nodded, biting my lip.

"Honey, Katie . . ."

My father interrupted softly. "Just get your stuff. We have to talk about Katie."

"I don't *want* to talk, I want—"

"Nancy, *please.*" My mother was crying now. Utterly confused, I went upstairs, threw my clothes, toiletries, and

Billy Bear, my teddy, into my blue duffel bag. I was pissed as hell at my parents, but confused—they were acting so weird. I didn't know how to argue with them. Until I could think of something good and nasty to say, I figured I'd go along with them and whatever they were planning.

A half hour later, my parents and I were walking down a white hallway to my shrink's office. "The Eminent Doctor Pear-Butt," I imagined the placard on his door said. Neither my parents nor I had uttered so much as a grunt since we'd gotten into the car.

"Nancy! Good to see you! How was your weekend?" Pear-Butt asked, too cheerfully, I thought. I wanted to give him a knuckle sandwich, as my grandfather used to say.

"Fine," I mumbled, slouching into one of the padded green leather chairs in front of his desk. My parents perched stiffly at the edge of the couch.

"You told her?" P.B. asked my parents, his bushy eyebrows rising over the top of his glasses.

Mom and Dad shook their heads.

Pear-Butt looked at me. "Nancy, this is maybe not the right place to tell you this, but your parents thought it best if maybe I could be here. They didn't know what you might do. Nancy, Katie died yesterday."

I stopped breathing. I slowly exhaled and, shaking my head just as slowly, I turned to look at my parents.

My mother nodded that yes, it was true.

I couldn't move or speak.

Getting up and coming toward me, my mother tried to smile compassionately. I thought I saw a hint of glee in her eyes—no more bad, terrible, evil Katie. That had to be what she was really thinking as she cautiously put her arms around me and whispered, "I'm so sorry, Nancy. I know you loved her very much. I'm here for you. I want to help."

"No!" I screamed, jumping from my seat and pushing her away. "No! No! No! . . ." I wanted to throw myself against the wall, beat my head on the desk, throw myself out the window, but instead I just kept screaming. I knew it had to be my fault. If I hadn't left her alone yesterday . . . if I hadn't let her do "dangerous narcotics," like the doctor said . . . if I hadn't . . .

"How?" I demanded, trying to assume some semblance of rationality, but unable to stop choking on my own breath.

"She fell out her window."

Memories of the previous day crowded into my head. It really *was* my fault, it . . .

"It wasn't your fault, Nancy," Pear-Butt said quietly. "She loved you. It was an accident."

I began to scream, first softly, then full force. My eyes squeezed shut. I didn't see my parents leave, didn't see the sedative coming until the needle had been in and out of my arm. I was sinking rapidly into a dark, blurred hole in my mind. Then, nothing. As I descended, I thought briefly, Katie. I'm going to Katie. I'm going with her.

Chapter 25

I was allowed to go to Katie's funeral with my parents, and then I went back into the hospital. For several weeks I refused to talk to anyone, and it was decided that I shouldn't go home again until I was more responsive.

My parents visited every Sunday. Because I refused to speak, they often brought books to read to me, or simply chatted at me about what was going on in Babylon. They even brought my schoolbooks, and I devoted myself to getting caught up with my work. This, coupled with a lot of introspection, helped me get over the shock of Katie's death. As my feelings of guilt and anger faded, I began to open up to the outside world again. This convinced my parents and the hospital staff that I was getting better.

Two days before Christmas, I was released from the hospital for good. After nearly four months of constant surveillance, the freedom was overwhelming. The first thing I did when I got home was call Mike.

"Nancy?" he asked, recognizing my voice. "You're home? That's terrific!"

"Yeah, it's pretty neat. So, what's up? Have you found a new girl yet?" I tried to sound carefree, although I was chewing my nails and hoping he'd say he'd been waiting for me the whole time I was in the hospital.

"I did start seeing a girl from school," Mike began, "but that didn't last long. I'm a free man now!"

I breathed a long sigh of relief. At least something in my

life remained unchanged. I could always count on Mike. "So," I said, trying to sound as seductive as I could over the phone, "wanna do something tonight?"

There was a brief pause, and then Mike answered, "Yeah, that sounds okay. I heard your old pal Amy is having a party. I'll pick you up at nine, okay?"

"I love you," I said out of habit.

Another long pause. "I love you too, Nancy. Sorry things had to work out the way they did. Maybe it'll be better this time around. Let's take it slow, okay?"

"Sure, no problem. See you at nine." I hung up the phone and noticed I'd bitten my nails down below the skin. My parents had gone to church, so I hurried downstairs to the liquor cabinet. It had been a long time since I'd gotten drunk, and I was in the mood.

To my horror, the liquor cabinet was filled with neatly folded tablecloths and a package of paper napkins. I stomped my foot. Damn them! I thought. Just because they wanted to go straight didn't mean they had to take the whole world along with them!

I went out onto the front steps of our house, lit a cigarette, and cried. Ignoring the cold, I thought, Oh Katie, where are you when I need you? I didn't even smoke the cigarette, but let it burn down to the filter while I stared into space and thought about Katie. The cold helped clear my head, and before my parents got home, I felt well enough to go back inside, take a shower, and get ready to go out.

Mike picked me up promptly at nine o'clock. "You look nice," he said as I got into the car, "Your hair is different."

I nodded. "I'm letting the color grow out. Black is too depressing. Don't I get a kiss?"

Mike kissed me lightly with closed lips.

I was pissed. I thought he'd be aching with passion the moment he saw me, but instead he concentrated on driving and making small talk.

Luckily, we were at the party in a few minutes and I had a vodka and tonic in my hand before I had a chance to blurt out anything I'd regret. Just keep 'em coming, I thought, gulping down the first drink. Keep 'em coming and everything'll be fine.

At eleven o'clock I crawled up the stairs to the bathroom on the second floor of Amy's house. By eleven-fifteen I was lying on my back in the bathtub, my dress covered with vomit, and my shoes in the toilet. I was just about to slip into peaceful oblivion when Mike came into the bathroom. With a wet washcloth, he cleaned me off the best he could, although my dress, which was red silk, was beyond saving.

"Like old times, right?" I said to Mike as he picked me up out of the tub. "Now we're goin' outside for air, like when we met, right? Startin' over?"

Mike didn't answer, but carried me out to his car, threw me across the backseat, and drove me home. When we got to my house I threw up again in the street and was deposited on my front porch. Mike rang the doorbell and left.

My parents let me sleep until three the next afternoon. By the time they yelled upstairs and ordered me out of bed, I was feeling much better and only had a small headache. I wonder what's in the refrigerator, I thought as I went downstairs. My parents didn't give me a chance to find out.

The kitchen smelled awful, and I soon found out why. In the sink lay my red dress, caked with vomit from the night before.

"After you clean that up," my mother said, coming into the kitchen behind me, "you can join your father and me in the living room for a family discussion."

Before last October, I would have taken that as a signal to put my shoes on and bike over to Katie's house. But of course, Katie wouldn't be there, and I knew my parents still had the power to send me back to the hospital, so I obeyed my mother.

My parents yelled at me for at least fifteen minutes. For the first time in my life, I sat still and listened. I thought a lot of what they said was bullshit, but I figured since they had the courtesy to let me sleep off my hangover, the least I could do was pay attention to what they had to say.

After a while, they stopped yelling and grew more rational. Then they asked me if I had anything to say.

"I'm sorry," was all I could think of. I knew I should be pissed that they were talking to me like I was a baby, but for the most part I thought they were right. I mean, I didn't have fun at the party. I didn't fix things with Mike. I didn't like throwing up or feeling hung over. And I'd ruined the only decent article of clothing I owned. Staring at the Christmas tree, all lit up and adorned with ornaments I hadn't helped to put on, I began to cry.

Even after screwing up at Amy's party, I knew I would be okay in the long run. Maybe not the goddess or saint my mother had hoped I'd become when she gave birth to me, but not the bad person I'd thought I was either. I hadn't known there was so much guilt in me before—guilt about not just what I did, but about what my parents, peers, Mike . . . everyone did. Even Katie. Slowly, I began to see that even she wasn't my fault. I didn't push her out that window, just as she had never pushed me. No one, not my parents or even myself, was to blame for anything. Shit happens, that's all.

New Year's Eve I sat in my room and stared for a long

time at the faint, white lines of a faded cross etched into my skin. I wondered if maybe that *was* the better way, if maybe by giving up cutting I was compromising myself and sinking deep into the suburban life-without-risks that Katie and I had always feared. I could almost hear Katie's voice saying, "We cut ourselves. It's what we are."

I couldn't go back to my old high school—too many ghosts and too much gossip. Instead, I enrolled at West Babylon High, one town over. By February I still hadn't made new friends, but I liked that. I enjoyed being anonymous. My self-imposed detachment allowed me to stay calm, and clear, and straight, most of the time.

Punk was kind of in by the time the new year, 1988, was rung in, at least in West Babylon. Whereas Katie and I used to stand out at Babylon High, suddenly I was seeing a whole crowd of girls sauntering through the halls, safety pins hanging from their ears and black spikes sticking up on their cropped heads. I almost felt like my mother when I wanted to say, "I was *you*. I *know* how wrong you are!" But most of the time I felt immensely jealous. Painful though it was, there *was* a lot of glamour to that kind of life. Sometimes I missed being a degenerate. Especially when I hurt so much inside my hands clenched and a familiar lump rose up in my throat.

It was the day after Valentine's Day when I got that feeling again, really badly. I went into the bathroom during second period to sneak a cigarette, and I got caught. First offense, so I was let off, but I still felt stupid. Later, during lunch, I went out to a local pizza place for lunch. I sat down at the Formica counter next to a girl from my English class. She had blond hair, cut in a crew cut, and the first time I saw her I was almost sure it was Katie, and everyone had lied to me—she wasn't dead after all. After that, I always tried to avoid looking at her.

"Hi," she said, blowing smoke in my face.

I had to look at her, so I smiled. She put her forefinger and thumb together and held them to her lips—a signal I knew too well.

God! It was *so* Katie! Shaking my head at the girl, I slid off my stool and hastily put my coat on, tearing the lining with the clasp on my bracelet as I thrust my arm through the sleeve. I went into the alley next to the pizza place and shivered in the cold, crying. Next thing I knew, the blond girl was next to me, offering a joint. I took it.

After school I had an audition for the school's drama club production of *The Hound of the Baskervilles*. Still flustered and a little high from my lunchtime experience *and* pissed at myself for smoking in the first place when my New Year's resolution had been to quit, I totally flubbed my monologue. I imagined everyone was laughing at me and ran from the auditorium to the bathroom. There I emptied my purse on the floor. I was in luck—stuck in a corner of the canvas bag was a small shard of glass. My emergency protection.

Biting my lip and crying, I gripped the glass and pressed it against my arm. But I couldn't move it. I wanted the lump in my throat and the pain in my head to go away, but I couldn't make the cut. I knew once I started I wouldn't stop, and all those months in the hospital would mean nothing. Katie's death would mean nothing. I stuffed all my garbage back into my bag. Still gripping the glass, I ran to the phone booth outside the front office.

Dialing my mother's number at work, I fingered the glass in my hand. "Mom?" I said when she answered the phone. "Mom, I want . . . I want . . ."

"Shh," said my mother. "Should I come get you?"

"I want *Katie*!" I cried, finally breaking down and blubbering. I dropped the piece of glass. I kept crying for several minutes, until slowly I felt the lump and the pounding in my head subside.

My mother was silent for a while. As my choking sobs quieted, she said, "Sometimes I want to drink. Right now, I'd love a cold glass of Dewar's and water. But I'm drinking a diet Coke."

I gulped and whispered, "Yeah. I know. I'm okay. Thanks."

"Do you want me to pick you up?"

"No. I'm okay. See you at dinner."

When I thought my face had lost some of its swollen redness from the crying, I wrapped my scarf around my head, put on my gloves, and slipped gently out of the phone booth. I smiled at a guy from my physics class and went to the parking lot for my car—actually my mother's old Chevette, in its last stages of life. I wasn't thinking about where I was going, but somehow I ended up at the cemetery. I sat in the car for a while, then finally crossed the frosty ground to Katie.

"Thank you," I said, kneeling on the ground and putting my arms around the stone. The granite felt like a block of ice against my cheek. "Thank you for everything. I miss you, Katie. Thank you for my life. I'll be happy for you. It's what you want, isn't it? Just tell me if it's not, okay? Just tell me anything I can do for you. I love you, Katie."

I continued to kneel by the stone for another half hour, and then went home. I wanted to call Mike, to see if maybe he wanted to catch a movie. I hadn't seen him since Amy's party, and I missed him.

About the Author

Shelley Stoehr was born in Pennsylvania and grew up on Long Island. In addition to writing, she also dances, choreographs, and teaches modern dance. Shelley Stoehr has performed at her alma mater, Connecticut College, and at the Laban Institute of Movement Studies in New York.

Crosses is an honor book in the Eighth Annual Delacorte Press Prize for a First Young Adult Novel contest.